Lowcountry Charm

STEPHANIE EDWARDS

Chapter One

APRIL 30, 1994

Tears roll down my cheeks. I wipe them with my free hand while holding my grandson, Clint. The oversized recliner cradles us, providing as much comfort as possible on the worst day in my fifty-one years on this godforsaken planet.

"Nana, why did Mommy and Daddy have to go to Heaven?"

How do I respond when I don't have the answers myself? I can't find my voice. The words are stuck in my tight throat, but I croak out, "Shh...baby. Please try to get some sleep. We'll talk tomorrow."

My heart races. I have to stay strong for Clint and his younger brothers. The reality stings—*I'm all they have now.*

His brothers lay asleep, too young to fully comprehend the loss they just suffered. Poor Clint knew the love of his devoted parents — my son, Wesley, and daughter-in-law, MaryAnne.

At eight, he was accustomed to the voices his dad made while reading bedtime stories, the sweet notes his mom included in his lunchbox and a never-ending supply of hugs and kisses.

Thanks to the carelessness of a drunk driver, the other boys wouldn't build those precious memories or bonds with their parents. I choke back a second round of tears and rub Clint's head until he falls asleep. His adorable little snores make me smile.

My little guys are down for the count. I don't want to take my eyes off them for a minute, but I can't stop yawning. After fighting a losing battle, I allow myself to drift off to sleep.

At midnight, I wake with Clint drooling on my arm. I hold the child tight as I stand and help him walk to his bedroom. Reminders of his parents are scattered everywhere. Framed family photos line the hallway walls, each memory and smiling face tugging at my heart.

When we reach his bed, I bend over to pull down his comforter. If his mama had known she had limited time with her babies, she wouldn't have wasted time on meaningless chores like making up beds. Instead, she would have held her boys close, covering them with kisses.

I'd give anything to watch her tuck the babes into bed even one more time. The boys stared at their mama like they knew she was an angel in disguise.

MaryAnne might have been my daughter-in-law, but I loved her as my own flesh and blood. When Wesley met her during their freshman year of college, they fell hard for each other. He announced they were engaged six months later, and I begged him not to rush into marriage.

But then, he brought her home over spring break to meet me. I could see why he cherished her. She glowed from the inside out and spent her spare time volunteering for every cause, from walking shelter dogs to visiting the elderly in nursing homes. To this day, I haven't met such a charitable young person. We clicked right away, and I vowed to welcome her into our family with open arms.

Becoming a mother didn't prevent her from helping others. As a pediatric oncology nurse, she gave more than she took in the world, comforting sick children and their parents.

She adored her boys. I'll always tell them how wonderful their parents were and show them the photo albums and scrapbooks MaryAnne painstakingly kept. Most of all, I'll shower them with affection. I could never replace her, but I'll love these young'uns with every fiber of my being.

I cover Clint with a soft quilt and brush my hand across his face—my perfect little guy. I shut off the light and check on the other boys in their rooms.

They're still snoozing and oblivious to the searing pain Clint and I are experiencing. Although they deserved to know their parents, I'm grateful they aren't facing this devastation. Two broken hearts are enough in this house.

There's no way I can fall asleep now. I wish I could call my best friend, Julia Caroline, but it's too late. Only the ocean's song can provide me comfort at this hour.

Stepping outside, I listen to the waves crash on the shore and take in the salt air with each deep inhale. A chilly breeze grazes my bare shoulders, and I shiver. I consider going back inside to grab a shawl, but I don't want to risk waking the children.

I plop down on a gray, weathered rocking chair, hugging myself to warm my arms. I try not to replay the call from Wesley's officers at the Isle of Palms Police Department from that afternoon in my head as I rock. But I keep hearing, "Ma'am, I'm sorry to inform you that Chief Parsons and his wife..." My stomach drops every time, just like it did the first.

Wesley was the youngest police chief in the town's history. I couldn't be prouder of him, or his commitment to protecting the island's people. And they loved him for it. The man made his mark early in his career.

The repetitive tide and rocking motion hypnotizes me. I could almost fall asleep out here, but I shouldn't. The boys might need me, and I wouldn't hear them. I'll close my eyes for a couple minutes, and go inside to check on them one more time before going to bed.

Focusing on breathing, I empty my mind, pushing all the negativity aside. For some reason, I can't help but think about

Carl, my late husband who abused me in every way. I suppose it's only natural for me to think of my son's father now, even though he bruised my body and my soul for more than a decade.

Carl's untimely death came with every emotion—sadness, apathy, and guilt for being relieved. Sure, he left me as the sole parent, but Wesley and I were better off without him.

"Hey, Nancy...Nan, wake up," a voice whispered.

Huh? Who was that? I shoot straight up off the chair and look around. Not a soul in sight. A tingle runs down my spine. I must have been dreaming.

I shake off my nervousness and stare at the moon's reflection in the ocean. No diamond compares to its shimmer.

Wesley and MaryAnne were proud to buy this beach cottage, even though it was in the shambles. They could see the potential, and they were right. The unobstructed ocean views alone made their sweat equity worth the investment.

I never thought I'd end up living in their exquisite home without them. My house is too small for five little boys. They just lost their parents. I can't take them away from their home, too. At least for now, we'll stay here, and I'll give them the best life I can. I'll have my hands full, but I love these young'uns. They're such a blessing to me.

We'll have fun spending days at the beach and crabbing from the docks on the Intracoastal Waterway. At night, I can cook anything we catch. We'll play card games and read storybooks together before bed.

A wave of pain accompanies the tide and washes over me. My stomach drops, and I suck in a deep breath. I'll never get over losing my sweet Wesley and lovely MaryAnne. The best way to honor them is to raise their boys to be good men.

If it kills me, I will make sure my grandsons have everything they need while rewarding their good behavior and hard work.

I'll encourage them to finish school and find their passions— whether that means going to college or pursuing a trade. All that matters is the boys are happy, healthy, and set up for success. More than anything, I hope they all find someone to cherish as deeply as their parents loved each other. Everyone deserves a life partner and romance.

Someone taps my shoulder, and I spin around, expecting to see Clint standing on his tiptoes. No one is there. *Is someone messing with me?* I shake my head at my paranoia. Life has been beyond challenging today, and I'm sleep deprived. My imagination and nerves must be on overdrive.

It's time to go back inside. I try to turn the doorknob, but it won't move. Did one of the boys lock me out of the house?

I press my face against the salt-covered glass pane at the top of the door. No sign of the kids. I don't want to wake them, so I climb down the steps from the back porch and walk around to the front door. It won't budge either. How odd!

What can I use to break a window? I grab a brick paver from the flower bed and return to the back porch, ready to throw it through the panes.

When I rear back, paver in hand, the door swings open. I try not to scream, reminding myself five little ones are fast asleep. Telling myself to calm down, I steady my shaking hands. I don't need an explanation for what happened. I just want to make it through the night. Everything will seem better after I get some shuteye.

Padding my way to bed, a burst of cool air chills me. I need to have a handyman reseal the windows. With all the salty air, beach houses often need extensive repairs.

Metal rusts, and wood rots much quicker at the beach, even compared to homes a mile inland. My frayed nerves have met a similar fate today. Losing my mind isn't an option. I'm not responsible for just myself anymore. I've gotta get a grip.

These kids need their nana to be healthy mentally and physically. I probably dreamed someone called my name. It's likely what felt like someone tapping me on the shoulder was really a Palmetto bug. Lord knows I've had more than my share of these enormous cockroaches crawl on me in my lifetime.

What happened with the darn doors? If only one had gotten stuck, I could blame the humidity. Wooden doors swell in their frames, especially in the South. But two at the same time? *Who ever heard of such a thing?*

I'm not a construction expert, but I've lived in the South Carolina Lowcountry my entire life. This isn't the norm. Something else is happening. I shiver.

What can I do to protect my sweet babes?

Chapter Two

After staring at the ceiling all night, I give up and get out of bed around seven. It's early but not an unreasonable hour to call Julia Caroline. She picks up on the second ring—thank goodness. I try to hold back tears as I run her through the previous night's unsettling events.

"Oh, dear! I have a few ideas, and I'll come over soon. I have the girls here today. Is it okay if I bring them with me?"

"Of course. It will be good for the boys to have a distraction, even if it's for a little bit."

We hang up, and I cook breakfast. The scent of pancakes and bacon fills the kitchen. I'll make the baby a bottle when he wakes up. I fill up our plates and wrap them in foil before going to check on the baby and wake up the older kids.

Clint helps the triplets pull on the clothes I set out for them. He's such a good kid and always helps with his little brothers. I will make sure he has a childhood. It would be easy to depend on him to lend a hand all the time, but he needs to have fun and play, too.

I kiss Clint on the forehead, and we go to the kitchen. The triplets follow behind. At four, they need a little boost to get seated. Their sleepy faces make me want to pinch their adorable chipmunk cheeks.

After I set down heaping plates of food in front of the boys, I pour apple juice into their glasses. Everyone shovels large bites of pancake into their mouths, without so much as saying a word.

I'm surprised at how hungry we all are until I realize we didn't eat dinner last night. *Oh, my God!* I was too stuck in my head to remember to feed the boys. I'm already failing these children. *Am I capable of being the parent they need?* It's been more than a decade since Wesley lived with me, so I've forgotten so much about taking care of a child.

Tears spring to my eyes, but I push them back, refusing to cry in front of the kids again. They don't need to see me upset. Instead, I fork out heaping bites of syrup-drenched pancake and bacon into my mouth, hoping to calm my nerves with comfort food.

The front door pops open to reveal Julia Caroline and her granddaughters. She locks eyes with me and shifts her gaze to the boys. Without either of us saying a word, she offers everyone juice refills and a second round of pancakes.

Unsurprisingly, they take her up on both. I whisper my thanks, and she winks at me. I need to talk to her, but it will have to wait until the children are preoccupied.

When I've cleaned my plate, I head straight for the baby's room. He reaches for me, and my heart swells. As I pick him up, the scent of baby powder fills my lungs. His blue eyes sparkle as he stares at me and giggles—my baby boy. He's one of my five reasons for living now, and I've gotta keep going for them.

After I change his diaper, I take him into the kitchen. The older children aren't at the table, but I can hear them playing in the living room. Julia Caroline washes and dries a plate, placing it on the drying rack.

"Well, that's the last one. I won't ask how you're holding up because I already know." She pulls me in for a hug and doesn't let go right away. "I'll stay as long as you want. James is at a medical conference in Wilmington this week, not that he'd keep me from being here..."

I won't refuse her offer to stay. With my best friend by my side, I feel slightly saner than yesterday, even though the bleak emptiness of Wesley and MaryAnne's absence haunts me.

Julia Caroline reaches for the baby, and he coos. His sweetness makes both of us smile. She is the baby whisperer and can make even the most colicky child happy.

A crash thunders down the attic stairs, and I jump to my feet. My heart pounds in my throat. *Are the kids okay?* They're terrified of the attic, so I can't imagine them going up there voluntarily.

I run to see what happened, bracing myself to find Clint at the bottom of the steps with a skinned knee. Rounding the corner, I grit my teeth. *Do we really need something else to pile on to our grief today?*

When I reach the staircase, none of the kids are around. A gust of air punches me in the face, the putrid stench of rotten eggs accompanying it.

If the kids aren't responsible for the crash, what the heck happened? I gulp but laugh at myself. I'm on edge, and my imagination is working overtime. I need to calm down and focus on getting all of us used to a new routine.

Still, I should check out the attic to make sure there isn't a raccoon or some other creature wreaking havoc up there. I climb the steps, steadying my breathing as I go.

The door at the top of the steps is open. I scan the room for anything that may have fallen, but all the boxes sit stacked in neat rows along the walls. Not a darn thing out of place. *Then, what did I hear?*

An icy blast of wind pierces my skin like needles. *Where is that coming from?* The sheer curtains flap in the breeze. *The window is open!* Wesley probably opened it when he organized the attic last week. No wonder we're hearing a bunch of rackets and smelling off-putting scents!

I rub my arms and close the window. Movement outside catches my attention, and I strain to determine what I saw. The bushes whip back and forth for a minute. *Is someone hiding behind the greenery?*

I hold my breath. *Should I run and call the police?* There probably isn't a point. The intruder could escape before they arrive. *Geez, who dares to mess with my family today?*

The shrubbery flutters again, and I jump. I open the window and climb out onto the roof. I've had enough.

"Whoever is down there, leave now! I've called the police. They'll be here any minute." Hopefully, my scare tactic works, and this slimy human being will run away, never to return.

The bush branches move, and I let out a scream. "Didn't you hear me? I said, 'Get!'"

An enormous gray and white striped Maine Coon Cat jumps out of the bushes, turning back to hiss at me. I laugh so hard that I almost fall off the ledge. Okay, I had that coming. It's time to get back inside and check on the kids.

I step back inside and close the attic window, shaking my head at my paranoia. No one's out to get me other than the neighbor's fat cat.

I'm sure he'll give me the stink eye next time I take the trash to the curb. I giggle at the thought. Somehow, I think I'll survive without Mr. Mittens' stamp of approval.

Pulling the curtains closed, a prickly sensation creeps up my arms. I double-check the window. Yep—it's closed. *What's that all about, then?* I feel someone's eyes boring a hole in the back of my head.

Did Julia Caroline come to check on me? No. She wouldn't leave all the little ones downstairs by themselves.

As I turn around, a large box launches itself into the air, and I scream. *How did that happen?* I run to the staircase, taking two steps at a time.

Out of breath, I search for Julia Caroline and the children until I find them in the family room watching cartoons. Everyone is laughing except for the baby, who is asleep in the playpen. A wave of relief washes over me—they're okay.

I sit down next to Clint on the sofa and catch Julia Caroline's eye. She stares at me, stands, and pulls me up. We walk back to the kitchen, where she pours me a glass of iced tea.

"Sit down. Now, spill the tea — not the Lipton I just poured you — but what's going on?"

I shift in my seat a couple of times. "I swear, I don't know where to start. I reckon I've gone off the deep end for real this time."

Julia Caroline grasps my hands. "Hon, we all have our moments. Try me."

I grit my teeth but share everything I experienced. "I know you went through your share of spooky hauntings when we were girls. But I ain't never... Do you think that's what is going on now?"

She stares at her slender hands. "To be honest, I was shocked you didn't see or hear anything strange when Carl died. He was such a horrible man in life, and I expected the worst from him when he died. I was grateful he left you alone and went on to his great reward, or wherever he went. But maybe he never moved on to the Other Side. If that's the case, I'm guessing the trauma of losing Wesley and MaryAnne opened up your gift to see and communicate with the dead."

My blood turns cold. I can't face my late ex-husband again, especially not with my sweet babes depending on me. I pull a quilted flannel shawl off the back of my chair, wrapping it around my goosebump-covered arms.

"What should I do?" I massage my forehead to prevent an impending headache. I would like to fly off the handle on his sorry butt, but Julia Caroline will have a much more sensible solution.

Julia Caroline frowns. "We're going to have to wait for that son of a biscuit eater to show his ugly face, so we can be entirely sure it's him. Until we know who we're working with, we could do more damage than good."

I groan. She's right, of course. We don't know that Carl is the one making my arm hair stand on end. Nothing menacing has happened yet, and that isn't his style. I have the scars to prove it and not just the kind you can see. These go much deeper.

We wander back to the family room to check on the children. It's time to make lunch, and I can't bear the thought of keeping them cooped up all day. I've never believed in letting a TV babysit a child, and we all need some fresh air.

I join the children on the couch and snuggle with them. "Hey, kids. Julia Caroline and I are going to make all of us a picnic lunch. We'll take it out to the beach. What do y'all think?"

Clint stomps the floor and screams, "I only want to go to the beach with my mama! It's not fair I can't go with her anymore." The triplets start crying, and I want to join them. I'm not strong enough to give these kids what they need. My heart has shattered, too.

Julia Caroline grabs my hand. "I'll go talk to the older boys. Why don't you go lie down with the baby for half an hour or so? If everyone is up to it, we can try to head to the beach again."

I pick up the baby and nuzzle him. *Yuck!* He's due for a diaper change, so I take him to his bedroom. After he's cleaned up, I place him in his crib and lie down on the daybed in his room. This is where MaryAnne and Wesley slept when the baby was sick or fussy.

With the mattress cradling my body, it's almost like a hug from them. I allow myself to drift off to sleep.

A short time later, the baby's cooing wakes me. I yawn and stretch. That nap really helped. I'd better go pack our lunch for the beach, assuming the boys are feeling better. If not, maybe ordering pizza and watching a movie will help take their minds off our problems.

I wander to the kitchen, and Julia Caroline is already making peanut butter and jelly sandwiches, cutting them diagonally and removing the crusts.

"You are heckin' amazing, lady! Are the boys doing okay now?"

She nods. "They took a little nap, too. Clint just came in here to check on you. He's afraid he hurt your feelings and wants to go to the beach with you."

I grunt. "Oh, my little sweetheart. I need to hug him."

Walking into the family room, I see the boys lying on their bellies watching cartoons. Clint jumps up and wraps his arms around my waist.

"Nana, I'm sorry. I love you."

"Honey, don't you worry about a thing. We're all having a hard time, and I'm so grateful I have you and your brothers. You make everything better for me. I love you." I kiss him on the forehead. "Do you feel up to going to the beach? We don't have to, but it could be nice to swim if you're up for it."

He nods. "Yeah. I wanna swim." I send him and his brothers to put on their swim trunks, and I return to the kitchen to help Julia Caroline.

She has set aside a large pack of fruit juice boxes, a party-sized bag of barbecue-flavored potato chips, and a sleeve of store-bought chocolate chip and pecan cookies. They're not as good as my homemade cookies, but they'll do.

We throw all the goodies and an oversized terry cloth picnic blanket into a couple of grocery bags and tell the children to put on some sunscreen before we leave. This will be good — no great — for all of us. I just know it.

Chapter Three

We walk to the beach and approach the glittering aqua-gray lapping waves. Breathe in, breathe out. Standing at the shoreline with the baby on my hip, the salt air fills my lungs and soothes my frayed nerves.

The older children splash and laugh at the water's edge. I smile—it's good to see them playing for the first time since the accident. Julia Caroline locks her gaze on them. I let out a deep sigh and spread out the picnic blanket, lying down with the baby by my side. The baby hasn't started crawling yet, so I'm not concerned about him getting away.

The sun's rays simultaneously blind me and send a warm rush through my body. I try to shield my eyes with a hand, a futile effort. *Why does the sun always sear my pupils like a steak on a grill?* I should have brought sunglasses. *How could I forget such a basic necessity?*

More than anything, I want to give in to the warmth and sleep. A beach nap would help me heal. *Listen to reason, Nancy.*

I check on the baby again. He's snoozing. *Would it hurt to fall asleep for a few minutes?* All the kids are safe with Julia Caroline.

Maybe I'll feel up to playing kickball with the older kids after I nap. I allow the sun to wrap me in a cozy cocoon and lull me to slumberland.

Letting go of the tension, I slide into a strange dream — an empty void. This is my first dream since Wesley and MaryAnne died. I'm not impressed. *Don't I deserve an uplifting distraction?*

Someone approaches me from the top of a hill in the distance. A black hood and the dark sky obscure their face. I stare, holding my breath. *Who is that, and why are they hiding?* The figure finally reaches me and pulls back the hood. I stumble backward and fall to my wobbly knees. I can't believe my eyes.

"Wesley?" I choke back hot tears. "Son, are you alright? I've missed you so much, and so has Clint. Wait...why are you here?" *Is this a figment of my imagination, or is he really here?*

Using his warm, firm hands, Wesley pulls me to my feet and twirls me around, transporting me to my garden. This sure feels real. The roses intoxicate me with their fragrance. Sunlight glitters across the grass.

Wesley lowers his head. "Mama, I..."

"Look, child. You know I want to see you, but it can't be good if you're here. You're supposed to be resting now. Is something wrong? Where is MaryAnne?"

"She's tending to other matters. Mama...somethin' bad is goin' on. We wanted to warn you."

My jaw drops. *Did I hear him right?* "Warn me about what?"

Wesley balls his fists. "Someone is after you. Please keep your eyes open for anything weird. We're so worried about you and the kids."

I blink, and when I open my eyes, we're sitting in Wesley's office at the police department. A chill tingles down my spine, and I shake it off.

"Who? Why would anyone bother coming after me?" I wrack my brain. I can't think of anyone who would want to hurt me. I live a pretty normal life for a Lowcountry grandmother.

He shrugs. "I don't know, but I've seen a shadow lurking

around the house. When it's around, the energy changes. It's like someone has sucked the life force out of our home. Mama, just be careful. I don't want anything to happen to you. Our boys need their nana."

My heart aches. Leave it to my son, the dedicated police chief, to patrol his home even after his death.

I grab his hand and lock eyes with Wesley. "I love you, child. I'll do everything in my power to protect your sweet babes. They're my whole reason for living. I'd take on an entire gang of hooligans to keep them safe."

He kisses my cheek. "I know you will, Mama. I'm sorry, but I have to go. MaryAnne sends her love."

His outline begins to fade, and the room spins, sending me to my living room. I reach out for Wesley, but it doesn't prevent him from vanishing into a mist. My arms collapse by my side, and I let out a scream. I've lost my loving son all over again. I can't control my tears this time. I wipe my eyes. My heart will never be the same after losing my boy or his sweet wife.

What I wouldn't give to rewind time, like a VHS tape, to an hour before they left for their date. I'd tell them to eat dinner at home instead. I'd cook for them and take the boys to my house for a pajama party. No task would be too great if I could bring them back.

Wesley and MaryAnne would have been able to see their boys grow up into fine young men — play sports, go on dates, graduate from high school, and find their place in the world.

That precious couple had so much more living to do.

But death doesn't work that way. She's a cruel mistress that steals the ones you love, never to give them back.

I wake covered in sweat and shiver as a frigid blast of air stings my lungs. I tense up — the boys! *Where are they? How could I fall asleep when something strange is afoot?*

Lost in panic, I jump when the baby coos. I pick him up, squeezing him tight to my chest. *Whew! Thank goodness he's okay.* I scan the beach for the rest of the gang. The other kids are burying Julia Caroline in the sand closer to the water.

Ever the trooper, she sings sea shanties as the boys dump buckets of sand on top of her torso and the girls follow behind with buckets of water.

I've never felt luckier to have this woman as my best friend.

Chapter Four

Three weeks later, the boys and I have mostly settled into our new routine. The baby and I spend our days together while Clint is back at school and the triplets have returned to preschool.

I'm still worried about them readjusting, but getting back to a schedule will help all of us. I decided to wait to return to my server job until the baby is old enough for preschool.

Being around will let me make sure the other kids are learning and having fun, especially with summer vacation starting in a couple of weeks. It's so important.

Thank the good Lord—money isn't a huge concern for us. I have saved my tips for the past few years, so I have a nice nest egg to cover our expenses for a while. Wesley and MaryAnne gave their kids a wonderful life but didn't spend a ton of money or leave us with a lot of debt. And they both had generous life insurance policies from their employers.

As the baby naps, I fold laundry and take little stacks of T-shirts to each boy's room. Clint's action figures tower over his dresser and the adjacent shelves. Navigating the rows of warriors and army men, I gently pull out a drawer and place the laundry inside.

Closing it back, I hold my breath. Nothing budges. I let out a sigh of relief and laugh. *Who ever thought I'd be worried about knocking over a plastic figurine?*

I turn to leave the room when fire shoots up the ball of my foot. *What on earth?* I look down to see an action figure under my foot. I move to step off it, but it moves with my foot. Another wave of searing pain radiates from across my arch to my toes.

Sitting down on Clint's wooden toy chest, I pull my foot up onto the other leg to examine it. Inside the figure's hands is the handle of a small pocketknife.

Gulping, I pull the toy away from the knife. The base of the blade is sticking out of my foot. I try not to scream. This is going to be a bloody mess. I grab one of Clint's clean shirts out of the adjacent dresser and brace myself for the impending horrific pain.

Squeezing my eyes together, I bite my cheek and pull on the knife in a smooth, quick motion to keep the blade straight as I pull it out. *Oh, my stars!* Giving birth to Wesley hurt, but at least I got a baby as a reward for that mess.

Before the blood gushes too much, I tie Clint's T-shirt into a makeshift bandage and pray I can make it to the hospital without too much drama.

I hobble to the nursery to collect the baby and a diaper bag. Slipping on my worn-out house shoes over the bandage, I lean over to pick up the baby. He wails, so I make sure his diaper is clean, and he had a bottle right before his nap. I can't take a crying baby to the emergency room.

Please, Lord, let Julia Caroline be able to take care of this young'un and round up the others from school and preschool. I call her, and the phone rings off the hook. Maybe she's outside gardening.

I don't have time to waste, so I fasten the baby in his car seat and drive the six blocks to her home on Palm Court. My knuckles turn white during the short drive, and I'm pretty sure I sweat out enough saline to build another ocean.

Both Julia Caroline and James's vehicles are sitting on the driveway. Relief washes over me, and I scream, "Thank God!" I need my friends and the good Lord more today than ever.

My pulse races, and I stumble as I fiddle with the car seat. We didn't have these darn complicated contraptions when Wesley was little, but I'm glad to keep the baby safe...if I can just figure out how to use it.

I finally wrestle the baby free, grab the diaper bag, and ring the doorbell. My legs wobble, and the pain shoots from the bottom of my foot to my knee. I look down to see Clint's T-shirt soaked in deep burgundy blood. *That can't be good.*

Heavens to Betsey! Why isn't Julia answering the door? I bang on the door furiously and begin calling out for my best friend, James, or anyone. I just need help!

Am I ill-equipped to take on raising five little boys? Is it too much for this old gal?

James comes to the door, wearing a bathrobe. *Oh, dear...I've disrupted a romantic escapade.*

Speechless, I start to back away, mumbling something about calling Julia Caroline later that evening.

But I feel my feet go out from under me. The darn slippers must have gotten caught on a rock. Clutching the still-wailing baby for dear life, I fall flat on my back. Sobbing, I try to catch my breath, but I can't. The baby's screams echo through the moss-covered oak canopy along the circular drive.

Everything goes black.

I don't remember James picking me up and taking me into their living room, but he must have. I'm sitting here now, in front of a roaring fire. *Oh, yeah—I definitely ruined a romantic moment.* I blush.

Then, I realize my arms are empty. I sit upright and scan the room. "Where's the baby? Did I drop him? Is he okay?" Sweat beads across my brow and I wring my hands.

Julia Caroline walks into the room with a cup of tea, shushing me. "Honey, he's fine. I gave him a bottle and put him in Brittany's crib." She pats my hand. "The question is, how are you, and how did you get that nasty gash on your foot?"

I look down at my foot. The worn-out house slippers and Clint's blood-soaked shirt are gone. In their place are a clean bandage on my injured foot and a bright white sock on my other.

"When did you clean up my foot?"

Julia winks. "James took care of it since he's the doctor in our house."

James—I slap my forehead. "I'm so sorry I ruined your rendezvous." *How humiliating! Hopefully, they'll forgive my awkward timing. I'll have to repay them somehow.*

"What?" Julia cocks her head, and her eyes light up. "Oh, no, nothing like that!" She laughs. "We went to the beach this morning and just got back. The water was a little cool for a swim, but you know that doesn't stop me when I'm determined! James lit a fire to help me shake off any lingering chills. He's making a pot of coffee to warm us up."

I laugh, too. "Well, I hope you still get to have a rendezvous all the same."

Julia Caroline shot a sly glance my way and waved her hand. "Oh, you, hush. Now, tell me what happened to your foot."

I wince as I share what happened with Julia. I fully expect her to tell me I've bitten off more than I can chew by taking in five children younger than ten. I don't want my best friend to confirm my suspicions. *Where would my poor boys go? And what would I do without them?* I shiver. That's the scariest thought to cross my mind.

Julia Caroline's expression changes from amusement to terror as I tell her about today's events. "So, the toy wasn't there when you went into the room. Are you sure it didn't fall when you closed the drawer?"

"I don't think so, but I can't swear to it."

Julia Caroline shakes her head. "I don't like you being there alone...not at all. James is going to have to be okay with me moving in part-time or y'all coming here to stay. We've got the room."

I put up my hand. "I can't let you do that. You have a husband and family to think about."

"Nonsense. James travels at least two weeks out of the month for medical conferences. The kids and grandbabies are only around every now and then. Most of the time, I'm in this big house by myself. Y'all would be doing me a favor by keeping me company. We need to get to the bottom of whatever or whoever is messing with you."

And if anyone can, it's Julia Caroline.

Chapter Five

James picks the boys up from school, and they thunder into Julia Caroline's kitchen full force.

Clint climbs into my lap. "Nana, why didn't you come get us from school? Are you okay?" He lays his head against my chest. His younger brothers cling to my legs like a herd of Velcro monkeys. A tinge of guilt hits me, but my heart leaps— *my boys need me.*

I tell them I cut my foot but don't go into details, not wanting to scare them. *Besides, what would I say? Your dead grandfather's malevolent spirit stabbed me with a pocketknife?* Shoot...no way. The less the boys know, the better. They don't need more drama in their lives.

Julia Caroline wanders into the room with the baby on her hip. "Are y'all ready to go home?"

I draw a deep breath but nod. *What kind of disaster will happen next? How can I protect these babes and myself?*

Julia Caroline pats my shoulder. "Don't worry. I'm coming with you for the night."

This woman always reads my mind. *I don't want to go home alone, but should I really let her come with us?*

I frown. "Are you positive James doesn't mind?" The couple just became empty nesters, with the last of their children graduating from college a few months ago. *Surely* James has romantic notions in mind with their newfound freedom.

"Not a bit—he leaves for Boston in the morning, and he'll be gone for a couple of weeks. Now, c'mon. These boys need some yummy dinner."

We head back to Wesley and MaryAnne's comforting home. As we enter the foyer, I can still smell the melt-in-your-mouth cinnamon rolls my sweet daughter-in-law enjoyed baking for her family. I hold my chest, trying to extinguish the pain.

The boys run past me, yelling at each other playfully. I smile, so glad they are feeling like themselves again. Nothing like boisterous little ones to make you forget your woes.

After letting them play for a little bit, I tell them they need to wash their hands and clean up their rooms. It's an adjustment going from being the fun grandmother to being their primary caregiver. But I'll treasure every moment.

Julia Caroline lays the baby down in his room. When she comes back to the kitchen, we start shelling creek shrimp and butter beans for dinner.

The repetitive motions of butterflying the shellfish relax me. It always has. Landlocked folks might gag while removing the slimy bits, but it's a way of life in the Lowcountry. And we know the sweet, salty reward that awaits us after we cook them.

A shrill screech followed by a bang comes from the baby's room. The hair on my arm stands on end, and my chest tightens. Julia Caroline and I make eye contact for a split second before we both run to check on the little one.

Thankfully, the baby is lying in his crib cooing. I fight back tears of relief and scoop him up into a tight embrace. After I catch my breath again, I look over at Julia Caroline. "What made that all that racket?"

She shakes her head. "I don't see anything out of the ordinary." Her face scrunches and her head pulls back. "Wait a minute..."

"What? Why are you making that face?"

Julia Caroline puts her hand on the baby's leg and stares at it with laser focus. I look down to see what holds her attention — a cluster of tarnished silver chain links wrapped around his tiny ankle. I grab his foot out of her hand.

The chain is familiar, but I can't remember why until my hand brushes against an attached round metal box. I examine the sweeping oak tree etched into the top and the wave pattern engraved into the sides of the circular charm and gasp.

"My mother's bracelet and prayer box charm! She loved this bracelet. I haven't seen this in years."

Mama believed the charm could pass messages from this world to the Other Side. I haven't ever experienced its magic myself, but she swore my Mee-maw stayed in touch with her after going on to her great reward in Paradise.

Where did the bracelet come from? How did the darn thing wrap itself around my darling little babe's ankle?

A cool burst of air grazes the back of my neck, and I shimmy to shake it off. *Did the person or being who moved the action figure do this, too?* The baby's coos and excited movements tell me no one hurt him. I let out a sigh of relief. *But why would anyone want to wrap a bracelet around a child's leg?*

I undo the toggle clasp and remove the greenish-silver links, lock eyes with Julia Caroline, and point at the charm. "Have you ever seen one of these?"

She nods. "My grandmother had one and used it regularly to call up our deceased family members. How did this one end up here, and on the baby's ankle, of all places?"

"I have no idea. I haven't seen it since my mother lived over by Breach Inlet." *Poor Mama.* She loved her one-bedroom beach cottage she bought with her own money after Daddy died. It wasn't much, but it was hers.

Sadly, she only lived there for a couple of years before she passed. I sold the place to a sweet young couple a year after Mama died. The only things I kept were the family Bible and my parents' wedding bands. I don't remember seeing the bracelet when I cleaned out the house.

Julia Caroline winced. "Where has it been hiding the past ten years?"

I shrugged. "I have no clue, but I've gotta see what's inside the charm. Let's open it!"

"Are you sure that's a good idea? What if there's a message to your mother in there? Or even worse, what if there's one for you?"

I wrinkle my nose. Julia Caroline is the voice of reason in our friendship. "I don't want to overthink this situation, or I'll chicken out. I don't have your decades of paranormal experience to help guide my decision-making. I'm just having to trust my gut and hope it's right."

I keep going and twist the latch on the intricately engraved silver box. Expecting something sinister to pop out, I hold the box away from us and take a deep breath.

A tiny pink scroll falls out of the box and rolls across the changing table next to the crib. I pick up the paper, holding it out from my body as if it's going to infect me.

Do I really want to read the note? I freeze in place.

Julia Caroline retrieves the scroll from my paralyzed hands. "Give it to me. I can't wait any longer." She unrolls the scroll and squints. "Oh, my word! You've gotta read this." She places the note in my hand.

I scowl, and Julia Caroline gives me a pointed look. *She's right.* My best friend always knows the medicine I need—to my dismay, she always makes me take it.

Sucking in air, I hold the paper up to the light and read the message aloud. "Someone is coming for you tonight."

What? The note slips through my fingers and hit the ground. *Who wrote this message and when? Was it meant for my mama or me? I wish I'd paid more attention to her superstitious ways and belief in magical trinkets.*

Julia Caroline grabs my hand. "I won't let anything happen to you or the boys. We'll figure somethin' out." I want to believe her. *How can she be so confident we'll be able to stop whoever is threatening me?*

Chapter Six

After feeding the children, I put their favorite animated movie in the VCR and set a puzzle box on the floor. That should buy some time for Julia Caroline and me to brainstorm a plan.

We go out to the porch, and I collapse onto a rocking chair. After everything our family has been through over the past month, we certainly don't need a riled-up spirit messing with us. What would anyone–alive or dead–want from me, anyhow?

Julia Caroline clicks her tongue. "Who do you think sent you this note? What does it mean?"

"I swannee. If it's not Carl, I can't imagine. I just want my boys to be safe. Nothing else matters. What can we do to stop whoever or whatever from hurting us or worse?"

"We're just gonna have to wait until this raging ogre shows their ugly face to figure out exactly what we're dealing with."

Ugh. When kids are involved, preparation is key. I don't like not having a plan.

The children's movie ends just in time for them to go to bed. I absent-mindedly tuck them in and kiss their foreheads. *Thankfully, Clint didn't ask for a bedtime story tonight.* He can read but still enjoys the nighttime ritual. I love reading to him, but I don't think I'd be able to concentrate on the words on the pages.

When I finish my nighttime rounds, I sit down in the kitchen and lay my head on the table. The coolness of the marble surface cools my flushed cheeks. For a menopausal woman living in the South, this might be the ticket to surviving hot flashes in the summer.

Julia Caroline checks on the baby one more time and grabs the baby monitor, so we'll hear if he cries. She sits down beside me. "There are some things we can do to at least protect ourselves. I'll gather up everything we'll need. While I do that, think through your favorite Bible verses and be ready to say them when I tell you."

I take a deep breath and think through the passages that have helped me through hell in the past. I'm convinced that Carl, my late ex, lived to torture me. I had the bruises and broken bones to prove it. I'm still weary from our past together.

Is he trying to punish me now because I broke our marriage vow, "Til death do us part?' When I divorced him to save Wesley's life and mine, did he intend to kill me? I shudder.

What an evil person. *Why didn't I recognize the signs of his manipulative, controlling, and emotionally abusive tendencies before we got married and had a child?* I could have saved all of us the pain during Carl's life and whatever is happening now…a haunting? My stomach sinks.

I silently recite Psalms 23:2. *"He maketh me to lie down in green pastures; he leadeth me beside the still waters."*

A calmness overcomes me as I remember I'm not in this alone. Of course, I have Julia Caroline, but God holds all of us in his loving arms.

I grab Julia Caroline's hand and bow my head in prayer, "Please, Lord. Watch over these babes and me as I raise them. They need me, and I want to give them a healthy, happy life. I want their parents to rest in peace, knowing their kids are thriving. In Jesus' name, Amen."

Julia Caroline wipes a tear from her eye. "Amen. I promise

you we'll find a way to protect you and your precious boys. I can't imagine if anyone was messing with my girls. But I do know we're two tough old crows. Whoever is responsible hasn't thought through who they're dealing with."

I squeeze her hand and sigh. "Sounds like Carl. He never paid my intelligence and know-how any mind when he was alive. Why would he after dying?"

Julia Carolina jumped to her feet and banged her fist against the table. "By golly ... we'll show him!"

My best friend doesn't scare easily, and come hell or high water, she is always ready to take on the most malevolent of spirits. She successfully sent her father-in-law's maniacal spirit to the Other Side after he threatened her and James' safety and wedded bliss.

Word about her gift spread around our small island, and many others came to her for help to banish raging ghosts to their final resting place. She even published a book on the subject when we were younger, but the big-headed mayor at the time banned it, saying the pages contained witchcraft. In reality, he was bitter over a personal matter.

It didn't matter, though. No one could take away Julia Caroline's power, knowledge, or courage. I'm fortunate to have her paranormal prowess and quick wit on my side. Especially now.

I'm at a loss for words or ideas for how to solve my conundrum. I know Julia Caroline will help.

Pacing the kitchen floor, she gazes off in the distance, mumbling under her breath. I know better than to disturb her when she gets like this. It's all part of her process. *Who am I to argue with anyone's proven ghost-hunting and busting methods?*

Julia Caroline stops in her tracks and locks eyes with me. "I know how you can prove who's messing with you. Don't say anything, just in case they're listening, but think about what would bother this person the most. You need to bait them with exactly that."

I squint, wrinkling my forehead. *What is Julia Carolina*

talking about? Has she slipped off her rocker? We're all a little kooky right now, so I'm not passing judgment.

Then, it dawns on me. She's asking me what would infuriate Carl beyond belief. He had a jealous streak a mile wide. I know the perfect thing to tee him off, and I'm only too happy to oblige. *Why didn't I think of this earlier?*

I run to my bedroom to grab my address book, and I call every eligible bachelor over the age of forty-five on the island. None of the first ten men I call answer, but no matter. I hadn't tried the one who would make Carl the most jealous—Brian Masterson, his childhood best friend. They spent almost every waking moment of the first seventeen years of their lives together.

Brian asked me out, not knowing Carl had a crush on me since we first met. I've never seen two nearly grown men act like such babies, getting into fistfights and loud arguments for weeks.

I should have run from both of them, but I dated Brian until I walked in on him kissing another girl. He didn't know I saw them. That night, I called him and broke off our relationship without giving a reason. I figured if he wanted to kiss someone else, she could have him. Cheaters are the scum of the earth, and I didn't want to set myself up for losing my boyfriend to some tramp.

Carl was waiting in the wings to ask me out. I'd always taken a shine to him, regardless of his brooding demeanor and anger issues. My teenage hormones didn't listen to my brain or my mama's warning.

There's no room for common sense when you're in love or lust.

After watching them beat each other into a bloody pulp more than once, I told Brian I'd never date him again, so he needed to move on. He disappeared for a week. I worried about him the whole time, but I couldn't bring myself to call.

When Brian returned to school, he refused to talk to either of us. Things only got worse when Carl gave me his mother's engagement ring. I heard rumors about Brian participating in risky behavior from cliff diving in the highlands near Greenville to drag racing in Darlington. I worried about his safety but figured I had lost my right to say anything when we broke up.

After graduating, James and Brian stayed in touch. Julia Caroline gave me updates when he moved to Atlanta for college and again when he moved back to the island with his new wife. I felt both relieved and jealous that he found someone new.

My life with Carl didn't exactly turn out the way I wanted. Seeing others with happy marriages stung, but I'd never admit that to anyone.

When Carl died, Brian came to the funeral. I was floored. Sure, it had been nearly two decades since high school, but things didn't end well between us.

At the funeral home, Brian approached me, offering his condolences until he saw the bruises up and down my arm. He stared at me, and I'll never forget the next words out of his mouth: "Looks like he's in a better place and so are you." He patted my shoulder and left.

Over the years, we've bumped into each other at church, the grocery store, and, well, everywhere—it's a small island after all. Our interactions were friendly but superficial. When his wife died, I felt horrible, but I couldn't get off work to attend the service.

During the last elementary school bake sale before Wesley and MaryAnne's accident, Brian and I kept cutting up with each other. At the end of the night, he asked me to join him for supper after church on Sunday. I've never been at a loss for words, but the cat must have gotten my tongue. Brian shrugged and handed me his phone number. I put it away and didn't look at it again until today.

I pound the numbers on the cordless phone, half of me praying the antennae has enough range as I paced the gosh-darned creaky floors, and the rest wishing for the worst. I hold my breath as the phone rings across a static-filled background.

One (crackle), two (crish), three (swish)...I should hang up— we're not gonna understand each other even if I get through.

Chapter Seven

"Hello? (crackle)."

I gulp. Should I hang up?

"Is someone there? (Swishhhh.)"

Get a grip—you're a grown, headstrong lady—no man can resist your sass or wiles. He's made it clear he wants to take you out to dinner, anyway. Use some charm and those womanly ways you've hidden for so long.

I force myself to smile, so I don't sound as scared as I am. "Hello, there. Nancy Parsons here. (Crash.) Did I call at a bad time because I can let you go?"

Brian clears his throat and my pulse races. "Hey. Not at all. I was (crish) you'd call. I've been out of town visiting my (crash) and her husband." He sighs. "I don't know how much you got out of what I just said with all the static. But I want you to know I was so sorry to hear about Wesley and MaryAnne. They were the best couple, and I'm sure going to miss both of them. Is there anything I can do for you or the boys?"

I draw a deep breath. "Thank you. I was hoping I (swish) take you up on that (crish) invitation."

Hiss. Crackle. Swish—darn island telephone lines are always messing up important conversations!

"Did I hear you right? Are you finally asking me out after all these years of me pining for you?"

I grit my teeth. "Am I too late to the game?" *What if he didn't want to go out with me now?* I try to convince myself I'm only disappointed because he'd provide the perfect bait for Carl's malevolent spirit. But deep down, maybe I have a little bit of a connection with Brian, too.

"Never. I'd love to have dinner with you. It's a date."

Choking on my own air, I can't stop coughing. This could only happen to me. When I finally catch my breath, I start laughing, which makes me cough again.

"I'd be worried if you weren't giggling, but that's a pretty sure sign you're breathing, and your ticker is tickin'."

"Oh, I'm fine and dandy—just a little embarrassed." Heat rises from my chest and up to my ears as I wipe my eyes with a tissue. Only I could make a fool of myself during my first semi-romantic call with someone other than Carl in more than thirty years.

"No need to feel embarrassed. How about we go out around seven tomorrow evenin'? Oh, does that give you enough time to find a sitter?"

"Yeah. The little ones will be winding down by that time. Anyway, Julia Caroline is stayin' with us for a bit. I'm sure she won't mind reading some bedtime stories and tucking in the babes."

I bite my lip, feeling a little guilty for not telling Brian the whole truth about our date. I push the pangs aside—taking care of my boys is worth telling a few white lies. Besides, Brian won't ever need to know about the haunting.

I'll do my best to keep all the spooky nonsense between Julia Caroline and me. No one else needs to be involved.

My thoughts turn back to the date. *What do I wear? Where are we going?* Brian didn't say. I'm too out of practice in the dating world to ask even simple questions. Goodness, what will us old fogies talk about?

I'm not one for being nervous, but trying to flirt is a little nerve-racking. Carl wasn't the romantic type, so I've never fooled with building those skills.

Julia Caroline wanders into the room. "I heard you talking to Brian. I had no idea there was *something* going on there. Why didn't you tell me?" She batted her eyelashes at me.

"Oh, hush, silly." I giggle. "He's a pretty good one to flirt with, though, right?"

She grabs her chest. "He's so dashing." I throw a decorative pillow in her direction but miss. "Don't get haughty with me, missy. I love the idea of you going out with Brian. He's a great guy. If you find a new beau and get rid of our unwanted pest, who am I to argue?"

I blink. At my age, finding a romantic match is a rarity, but not impossible. Does adding five adorable little but sometimes rambunctious boys to the equation change that?

In theory, Brian knows my situation, so he wouldn't agree to go out if it was a problem. But has he given it enough thought? He raised a family with his sweet wife, Lorna, God rest her soul. If we get into the thick of a relationship, and the boys are always around, he might decide he doesn't want to be a father figure again.

Julia Caroline waves her arms. "Earth to Nancy. I know you're overthinking this date. You need to at least give him a chance. Besides, it's just dinner, not a marriage proposal." *True, but did she climb into my head when I wasn't looking?*

I shake my head. "Are you telepathic? You always read my mind. I love you, but you're so darn frustrating like that!"

"I try my best." Julia Caroline fluffs her shoulder-length brunette curls.

"There are no words." I laugh. "Now help me figure out what to wear. He didn't give me an inkling of where he's taking me, so your guess is as good as mine."

She strikes a pose and puckers her lips. "We're going to make you look marvelous."

Chapter Eight

Late the next afternoon, I wrestle with the lace collar on my mauve floral dress while standing in front of the vanity mirror in my bedroom. The darn thing is determined to fly away. I don't blame it—I don't want to go on this date, either. But the linebacker-worthy shoulder pads have anchored the dress to my body.

As for me, Julia Caroline threatened to kick my butt across the island and back if I dare try to skip out on Brian tonight.

"Wipe that scowl off your face right now, Nancy Lynn Parsons!" Julia Caroline slaps my arm. "This is for your own good and your boys. Besides, all you need to do is eat and be polite. Is it sheer torture to have dinner with a man?"

I groan. "No—I'm just too old for this mushy stuff. Brian's a great guy. He'll probably decide he'd rather have a younger woman, and that's totally fine by me. I'm not fighting for anyone anymore."

Julia Caroline smirks. "You're blushing. Could you be more transparent? Obviously, you have a thing for him, and it sounds like the feeling is mutual. I'm excited for both of you. Now, put on your pearls and lipstick like a proper Southern lady." She gives me a gentle push.

I roll my eyes. "Since when have I worried about being a proper anything, well, other than a mother and grandmother? Besides that, I don't worry about what anyone thinks."

"Exactly. That's why you need to hurry and finish getting ready. You're an independent woman, living your life the way you want. This is your chance to prove all those people who say you can't find love after forty wrong, especially that old polecat, Carl."

"Love" wasn't a word I'd considered when planning the date. Instead, it makes my stomach churn.

At most, Brian and I might become close friends who meet for dinner, maybe watch a movie, or attend a church function together. If things went really well, we might be friends who kiss... certainly no more than that.

As I turn to share my thoughts on the matter with Julia Caroline, a whirring sound fills the room, and a cool breeze grazes my neck. I look up to see the ceiling fan spinning so quickly that the blades are almost invisible. *Who turned it on?* It's next to impossible to reach the cord to turn on this indoor tornado. I usually use a step stool. Julia Caroline is even shorter than me, so I know she didn't.

She shivered. "Why did you turn that thing on? It was already freezing in here."

"I didn't. Do you think I could reach that without some help?"

Julia and I look at the fan at the same time. The blades wobble independently instead of their usual synchronized arcs, and the gentle whir turns into the overpowering reverberation of a helicopter. *How am I going to shut it off without taking a beating?*

I grab a heavy cable-knit cardigan and throw it toward the fan, slowing the blades some but they continue to flop at erratic angles.

Julia Caroline draws a breath. "We need something heavier." I pull the poly-filled comforter off my bed and wait for the right angle to pummel it into two of the blades. The cyclone slows to an erratic rocking. This is my moment—I pull my step stool over and stretch toward the flailing cord.

Teetering on the edge of the stool, I finally reach the cord after several tries. With one final wobble and whir, the fan stops.

My legs almost collapse underneath me as I step down onto the floor. I let out a deep grunt and place my hands on my knees to regain my composure. I'd better check on the boys one more time.

Julia Caroline pats my hand. "Thank goodness you thought so quickly! I'm glad that's over."

"Me too." As I turn to look at her, a searing pain fills the right side of my body. Everything goes black and silent, but I refuse to give in to the darkness. There's too much to do before Brian arrives. I try to get up, but my vision blurs.

I feel a hand on my shoulder and someone telling me everything will be alright. The voice doesn't belong to Julia Caroline.

"Who said that?" I rub my head and open my eyes.

Julia Caroline places her hands on my shoulders and looks into my eyes. "Who said what? I went to get the cordless phone just in case you needed to go to the hospital."

"Never mind. I don't know what I heard." Great—now I'm hearing things. *Just what I need.*

"Are you okay? Do you need to see a doctor?" I decline, and Julia Caroline continues rattling off questions, clearly trying to make sure I have my mental faculties in place.

"No need for the third degree. I'm fine. Stop worrying. I need to finish getting ready and check on the kids again before I leave."

I pull myself upright and smooth out the crinkled edges of my collar. Glancing in the mirror, I tuck flyaway hairs behind my ears. A dark shadow appears over my shoulder, and I scream. The fan incident could be explained away as a freak accident or faulty wiring.

The voice I heard could be chalked up to an overactive imagination or a bonk on the head. *How do I explain the shadowy figure? Did I imagine it?*

"That's it! You're zoning out. I'm calling Brian to cancel your date this minute, and we're going to the hospital. Do you think you can change into some lounge clothing on your own? You never know how long we'll be in the emergency room."

I shake my head frantically. "We can't leave those kids with anyone else right now, and I don't want them worrying about me any more than they already are after yesterday. They've been through so much. But I think rescheduling my date with Brian for tomorrow is a great idea. I'll call him myself, so he doesn't worry, either."

Julia hands me the phone. "I guess you got your wish to stay home."

I narrow my eyes. "Maybe. But I wish the events leading up to this decision hadn't been so dramatic. What is this, Broadway?"

Chapter Nine

The following evening, Brian shows up five minutes early. I appreciate punctuality, but tonight my nerves are all over the place.

Before I answer the door, I close my eyes and count to five. I hold my breath as I open the door to see Brian wearing a beige linen suit and carrying an overflowing bouquet of yellow and white daisies.

"Thank you! How did you know daisies are my favorite?" I can't help but smile as he hands the flowers to me. Maybe this won't be so bad.

His eyes glisten. "I'll never forget you talking about the ones that grew in your mother's garden. You always looked so happy, so very beautiful, just like you do now."

My cheeks flush. *How could he remember such a trivial bit of information from high school?* I can hardly recall what I had for breakfast today, let alone a conversation I had during sophomore year. Butterflies swarm my stomach and flutter their way into my throat.

I'm too dang old to feel like this. They're just flowers, not an engagement ring.

Julia Caroline joins us in the living room, says hello to Brian, and takes the flowers from me. "I'll find a vase for these. Y'all have a great time tonight, and Nan—don't rush home on my account. The boys are asleep, and I'm gonna curl up with a good book in my room, so I won't hear if you come back in for a...uh nightcap." She winks at me.

Being on my best behavior, I let Julia Caroline's insinuations go. Instead, I thank her and follow Brian out of the house. As the sand and seashell driveway crunches under my feet, I feel like someone is staring at me.

I turn around; no one is there, not even a stray cat. The hair on the back of my neck stands up. *Is it a bad case of nerves, or is someone following me?*

Did creepy ol' Carl already take the bait?

Taking a deep breath, I push the thought aside and continue walking to Brian's sleek black sedan. My pulse races. Now isn't the time to worry about having a stalker. I have a more pressing matter to consider—how to get rid of my sweaty palms without being obvious.

Brian opens the passenger door and smiles. "I'm so glad you're feeling better."

I force a weak smile. "Me too." My heart pounds as I get into the car. *Why did I let Julia Caroline talk me into this?* Brian is a nice guy, but I have no idea what to talk about on a first date. *What if he wants to kiss me goodnight?* It's been so long since I've entertained such a notion.

Brian joins me in the car and grins. "Are you up for something a little out of the ordinary?" *How am I supposed to respond?* I give up on being nonchalant about my sweat-drenched palms and wipe them on my dress.

"Umm..." I grit my teeth. I don't like surprises, not even on my birthday.

"Nancy—do you trust me?"

"Mmmhmm..." Brian is trustworthy. I have to at least give him that. "Of course. I've known you since I was knee-high to a grasshopper."

He grabs my hand and leans in close. "I won't be mad if you want to get out of the car now and go back in the house. But please hear me out. I promise you'll like where we're going. If you want to come back home at any point, I'll bring you right back. What do you say?"

I sigh, remembering the reason I planned the date. "Okay. Let's go but just for a couple of hours. I need to get back to check on the boys."

"Yes, ma'am. You have my word." He raises his right hand and places it on an invisible Bible.

As the car backs out of the driveway, I let my shoulders relax. *So, what if I say the wrong thing to Brian?* It doesn't matter in the least. I haven't been on a date in decades, and I won't complain if I never go on another.

Brian turns on the radio, and a familiar song fills the car. I hum along, but after the first couple of bars, I realize it's the song Carl declared to be ours. My stomach sinks. *Why did I let that evil man charm me?*

Why is that song playing now of all times?

I don't want to make a big fuss to Brian. I try to change the station, but the radio dial won't budge. Well, that's just fantastic.

There's nothing I can do about the busted radio dial, so I let my head fall back against the headrest and crack a window. The cool breeze refreshes me.

As we cross over the lush green marsh along the Ben Sawyer Bridge to the mainland, the undeniable earthy scent of the pluff mud and the saltiness of the brackish water filters into the car and my lungs. These scents ground and comfort me. They are all I've ever known.

My gaze moves from the green spartina marsh grass to Brian. *Is he nervous, too?* He taps the steering wheel in time with the music while wearing an ear-to-ear grin like a teenager in love.

No sign of nervousness. Apparently, I'm alone in my anxiety. *Ugh.* No surprises there. *Why do matters of the heart and dating always come easier to men?*

Brian looks me up and down before turning back to the road.

"You look pale. Do you feel okay? Should I turn around and take you home?" I check my reflection in the rearview mirror—ghastly white.

Why can't I just enjoy a rare child-free night out with an old friend without being so dramatic?

I start to respond to Brian, but a flash of light in the mirror catches my eye. I do a double take. Fog covers the surface. *What the heck?* It's especially odd considering the mild weather and our windows being cracked.

"Hey, Brian. Don't you think it's weird that your mirror is foggier than the marsh after a storm in July?"

He gawks at the mirror as if it's sprouted wings. "Well, I'll be."

The fog begins to fade, revealing something underneath. I wince and refocus my eyes to see someone staring at me! It must be Brian's reflection being distorted in the fog.

But the smokiness has almost dissipated, and Brian's eyes are locked on the road. *Who is it then?*

I know the answer, but that doesn't mean I have to like it. Diverting my gaze, I close my eyes and take deep breaths as quietly as possible. *Here goes!* I look back at the mirror just in time to see Carl smirk before he disappears.

I jump in my seat. "Where in the 'H-E-double-hockey-sticks' did that son of a gun go?"

Brian wrinkles his nose. "I've never heard anyone call fog by such a colorful name before. Did you see something else out there? Are you sure you're up to being out tonight?"

If Brian doesn't think I'm a nut yet, he's bound to now. Maybe he isn't wrong. I'm wondering if I've finally lost it. That's the only logical explanation.

Chapter Ten

After reassuring Brian and myself I want to continue our date, I sit quietly. Carl's appearance wasn't a surprise…it was all part of my plan. At least I've confirmed the identity of my stalker. *But what will he do next?*

"Almost there." Brian flashes a smile.

Oh, geez. I haven't paid a lick of attention to where Brian is driving. If he turns out to be an axe murderer, I guess I'll be shark bait in a matter of minutes.

I lean out the window to take in some fresh air and orient myself as the sedan rumbles down a dirt road. Brian pulls up to a small white house on stilts and parks beside a grand oak tree dripping in Spanish moss. He gets out of the car and opens my door. My feet wobble slightly underneath me, but I regain my stance.

"Whoa, there. Are you really okay?"

I bite my lip. "For a given definition of the word. But don't worry. I can at least make it through dinner. I want to catch up with you tonight."

He nods, grabs my hand, and leads me behind the house. Party lights wound across the dock railing shimmer on the Intracoastal Waterway. At the end of the dock sits a cafe table and chairs for two with beautiful stemware and a bottle of expensive champagne chilling in an ice bucket. There's something familiar about this place.

The gentle breeze grazes the back of my neck as I cross the squeaky deck boards. Stars and a crescent moon paint the sky with their glow.

"What do you think?" Brian places his hand on my shoulder. "Do you remember my family's old homestead?"

How could I have forgotten this place? Memories flood my mind, and I go back to a simpler time in my life. I was fifteen years old, slim, and not afraid of a darn thing.

While sitting in homeroom, Brian waltzed in, wearing his skintight white T-shirt and jeans. I'd known him since we were children, but that day…that T-shirt…those jeans…his baby blues… whoa! I was smitten.

I couldn't take my eyes off Brian as he plopped down at the desk in front of mine like he had every day before that year.

Wearing a dazzling grin, he asked me out. I had to bite my tongue not to squeal.

After weeks filled with the quintessential teenage dinner and movie dates, Brian asked me if I was okay with hanging out at his house instead. I didn't care where we spent our time if we were together.

Many afternoons, we lay on this very dock, contemplating our future. It looked quite different in the daylight—I never stayed until dark. My daddy would have pitched a fit.

Those were purer times, when a couple waited until marriage to make love. Parents did everything they could to keep their children's relationships above the board. Many older folks thought allowing teenagers to be alone in the dark was a recipe for promiscuity. There isn't anything you can do at night that you can't do in the broad daylight. But I had too much respect for myself and my parents' wishes to break my vow of celibacy until my wedding night.

As a rule, I only gave in to temptation when it came to sweets. Brian's mama, God rest her soul, made the most sinfully delicious peach pie and homemade vanilla ice cream I've ever devoured. I enjoyed my conversations with her dearly and even envisioned becoming her daughter-in-law. I think she anticipated me becoming part of her family, too.

If I hadn't broken up with Brian, my life would have been different. For one thing, I wouldn't be in this precarious spot with Carl or had to deal with all the pain he inflicted.

But I wouldn't have had the best gifts of my life—Wesley, his sweet MaryAnne, and their precious boys. Time with them is all that matters.

Brian drops his hand from my shoulder and grabs mine, bringing me out of my trance.

"I thought we could have dinner out here tonight and talk about old times. My youngest daughter set everything up when I left for your place." He pulls out my chair, and I sit down, soaking up the scenery. The draping Spanish moss whips in the wind, casting an eerie shadow across the illuminated section of the dock.

I shiver. No matter how long I live in the Lowcountry, I'll never get used to that gorgeous but haunting sight—something straight out of a horror movie. Tonight, I'm more on edge, so that doesn't help.

Brian pulls a cooler from underneath the table and retrieves two foil-wrapped plates. He uncovers them and places one in front of me. My stomach rumbles at the sight and aroma of an overflowing pile of fried creek shrimp accompanied by grilled squash and pimento cheese grits.

"That looks scrumptious ... I see your daughter inherited your mama's cooking talents."

He grins. "She sure did. Just wait for dessert."

"Oh, boy. I'm glad I wore a roomy dress instead of tight pants for this date." Maybe that wasn't the sexiest statement, but I am who I am. If Brian wants to date me, he may as well get used to my honesty.

As we feast and talk, I almost forget about being nervous, Carl's antics, and the horrific pain I've experienced since the accident.

Brian grabs my hand. "It's so wonderful to have you here with me tonight. I didn't know if I'd ever see you on this dock again after you broke up with me. I had a blessed life with my Lorna and our girls. We made every minute count. But I've always wondered why you left me for Carl."

I'm transported back to my junior year in 1959 at my locker in Mount Pleasant High School. Brian always met me there before lunch until that fated day. I looked in the cafeteria, parking lot, empty classrooms, and even the gymnasium. When I didn't find him, I figured he must be at home sick. His home was just a short drive from school, so I begged my older brother for a ride. What I saw when we got there destroyed me.

I clear my throat. "I saw you sitting on the side porch kissing a big-bosomed girl I didn't know. I couldn't imagine kissing you after that. So, when Carl asked me out that afternoon, I decided to move on. I should have talked to you first, but I was a stupid, impulsive child then."

Brian blushed. "What? No—I'm so sorry. I wish you'd told me. Her parents were best friends with mine, and they were staying with us that week. Mama asked me to stay home from school that day to entertain her. I had no idea she would kiss me, and I didn't kiss her back. I told her I had a girlfriend, who I intended to marry."

My stomach flip flops. A misunderstanding forever changed the course of our lives. What a romance we could have had.

I wince. "I feel rather silly now. Not that we can change anything, but I can't help wondering what things would be like if we'd stayed together."

Brian kisses my hand. "It's not too late for us, Nancy. If you want, we can get to know each other again and see where things go. We're still young enough. We don't have to go through life alone."

I sit in silence. *What can I say—there are five little boys asleep in my house. Does Brian want to raise children again?* I couldn't blame him if he said no. At this point in our lives, most people are thinking about retirement and traveling or finding another thrilling hobby. Surely, he has plans to spend days on a golf course or at the beach.

"Brian, I enjoy being with you. But my grandchildren need me. I'm grateful for the opportunity to raise them, but I don't expect anyone else to sign up for the task."

"Please don't assume I wouldn't be up for it. I love kids, and none of my daughters plan to start families anytime soon. I would love to help with the boys and be part of their lives. They're great kids. I've always enjoyed seeing them out and about with Wesley and MaryAnne. Couldn't we give this a shot?"

He isn't the same boy I fell for in high school but a more mature, better version of himself. After getting so worked up over the date, Brian put my mind at ease and even helped me enjoy myself. We stand a chance to rebuild at least a friendship. Maybe more.

"Nancy, please say something. I'm dying here."

I laugh. "Don't do that. I'd like to continue spending time together and see what happens. All I ask for is complete honesty. If either of us wants to be only friends at any point, we tell the other one. Okay?"

"You got it, but is it alright if I kiss you now? We'll never know if we want more if we don't try."

I nod and the butterflies swarm my stomach once again as Brian leans in closer and gently presses his lips against mine. A warmth radiates throughout my body, and I lose myself. In this moment, I'm fifteen years old again, sitting on the dock flipping my feet back and forth in the water and stealing delicate kisses from the guy of my dreams.

"Wow..." Brian let out a deep breath.

My face reddens. "I know. I had forgotten what that feels like. We don't have your parents here to keep us honest tonight, so you'd better take me home."

"But not without dessert." Brian protested.

I glare at him and shake my head. If he thought I'd do that after one kiss on the first date, he couldn't be more wrong.

He holds out his hand. "No! Not that, silly. Actual dessert—

my mama's peach pie that you loved so much as a girl. Remember, I told you my daughter made it for us."

I cover my eyes and peek through my hand. "How embarrassing! We definitely don't want to forget to eat a piece of that luscious pie."

He cuts each of us a piece of pie and pours a couple of glasses of champagne. After handing me my champagne, he holds out his glass. "To us, Nancy Parsons, and to our future...whatever happens. At least we'll know we tried to find happiness together."

I clink my flute against his and take a small sip. The fizzy champagne tickles my nose, and I sniff, trying not to sneeze. I almost don't notice as the stemware crumbles in my hands, sending champagne and shards of glass everywhere.

The little hairs on the back of my neck stand on end, and the gentle breeze transforms into a full-blown gust. I suppress a scream as Carl's iridescent apparition appears beside me, glares, and shakes his head before disappearing into a glistening mist. My heart pounds furiously, and I want to yell at him. *Did Brian see him, too?*

Brian jumps up and runs to me. "Are you okay?" He examines my hands and arms.

I nod but can't speak. I can't tell him Carl broke the glass. *What if he doesn't believe in spirits?* That won't be a great way to end our first date.

Brian holds up one hand and places the other across his chest. "I have no idea what happened. My family has used those flutes for years...anytime one of my girls has had something to celebrate. I've never seen a glass crumble like that—almost like someone wadded it up in their hands like a piece of paper. How strange!"

He picks up the pieces of glass and hands me a kitchen towel to mop up the champagne on my dress. Too bad I can't clean the memory of Carl's face out of my brain.

I need to learn how to prevent the panic that sets in every time he appears or causes chaos.

<h1 style="text-align:center">Chapter Eleven</h1>

On the way home, Brian makes small talk, but I can tell he's trying to figure out what the heck happened on the boat dock. I want to explain, but I know I can't, at least not this early in our relationship.

I thank Brian for a delightful evening and agree to see him again. Before getting out of the car, I lean over and kiss his cheek. He's more than worthy of a second date. I need to draw Carl out of his hiding place for longer than a few seconds, so I can send him away to the Other Side for good. I make a mental note to ask Julia Caroline to give me a surefire way to kick his sorry butt.

When I open the front door, I see Clint sitting on the staircase that leads to his room.

"Sweetie, what are you doing out of bed? It's way past your bedtime."

He jumps up and runs into my arms. "Nana, where did you go? I had a nightmare that you died in a wreck like my mama and daddy. I was afraid I'd never see you again!"

My heart sank. Poor sweet boy—his parents went out one evening and never came home. Maybe it was too soon for me to leave him and his brothers with someone else, even though they think of Julia Caroline as a surrogate grandmother.

Patting his back, I promise him it was just a bad dream. "Honey, I'm not going anywhere. I just had dinner with a friend of mine, Mr. Masterson. Would you be okay if I invited him to come over here and have dinner with us sometime?" In our tight-knit community, those of us who live or work on the island know each other well. Brian lives in neighboring Mt. Pleasant but operates a small coffee shop a couple blocks off the beach. He knows Wesley and MaryAnne's boys well from church and school events.

Clint nods. "I like him and his magic tricks." I coughed to hide a giggle. Of course, Brian's sleight of hand tricks are famous on the island. All the kids love watching his incredible performances. Heck, so do most of the adults.

"Wonderful. We'll see when he has time to come over for a fish fry. Now, we need to get you back to bed. Ready?"

He walks upstairs and puts himself back to bed. I pull the covers up and kiss his forehead. "Goodnight, sweetheart. I love you."

"I love you, Nana."

I beam. I'll never tire of hearing those words from my precious boys.

I walk into the hallway and turn around to close the door behind me. The weight of someone's gaze gnaws on my nerves. I pivot quickly, ready to give Carl a dose of his own medicine. Instead of a ghoulish figure, Julia Caroline stands there with a mischievous grin across her face.

"So, did that snake Carl have the nerve to show his ugly mug tonight?"

I fill Julia in on the chilling scene on Brian's dock and beg for a solution to end Carl's haunting.

"What's it gonna take to send Carl on to his great reward for good? I'm done with these casual pop-ups he's making a habit. Doesn't he know a lady deserves at least a day's notice before a gentleman caller shows up? Not that he's ever been a gentleman."

"Nan, you're going to have to teach this evil spirit a lesson, and it won't be easy. I need you to keep seeing Brian and learning more about Carl's strength." She pauses. "Will that be okay? I know you weren't thrilled about going on a date, but if it's for the wellbeing of the children, I'm sure you'll do whatever it takes."

My ears and cheeks burn. "I think I'll be alright going with Brian however many times it takes. Maybe even more."

Julia Caroline's eyes widen, and as she claps her hands together and looks up. "Please, Lord, tell me it's true—you've helped our sweet lil' Nancy find the man of her dreams. Rain blessings down upon them. In Jesus' name. Amen."

"Stop all that now. We're seeing where things go, but we've decided to be friends for now. If we become more, that's great; if not, that's okay, too." I fan myself, trying not to let Julia Caroline see my reddening face.

"Can't I pray for my best friend's happiness?"

I sigh. "Of course you can, but if it's God's will, we'll end up together. I'm positive of that. So, let's pray for Carl to leave this earth because until that happens, I'm going to have a difficult time focusing on another man with all my heart."

Julia Caroline nodded. "I'll think through all this. I'm sure we can figure it out."

"Yep. Well, at least we know who we're dealing with and how to rile him up really good. I know how to push all that jerk's buttons. Lord knows he deserves it after the torment he put Wesley and me through when he was alive."

Julia Caroline pounds her fist. "That's what I like to hear, and I'd love to talk about it more tomorrow." Her voice trails off in a yawn. "Sorry about that. Let's get some shuteye. I'm about to conk out while standing up. 'Night, Nan." She hugs me before going into the guest room and closing the door behind her.

I'm ready to go to bed, too, but after this wild night, I doubt I'll fall asleep anytime soon.

I go into my bedroom, lie down, and proceed to toss and turn on the soft mattress. Finding a comfortable position is proving to be impossible. It's no wonder—I went from living the boring life of a grandmother who worked an ordinary part-time job as a waitress to having five live-in grandchildren, a dead ex-husband who wants to murder me, and an old flame that is being rekindled. Most people's lives don't go from zero to sixty quite that fast.

After hours of rolling from one side to the other, I finally drift off to a dreamless, peaceful sleep—something I've longed for ever since the accident.

When I wake at 4:30 a.m., covered in sweat, Wesley is on my mind. I'm unsure why, but I don't need a reason. A mother should never bury their child. It's the wrong order of things. When it's your only child, the sting is so much worse. I'm only grateful we never left things unsaid. Wesley and MaryAnne knew I loved them. Even more importantly, Clint and his brothers knew their parents' unconditional love.

"I promise you, Wesley and MaryAnne—I'll always take care of your boys." I blow a kiss up toward Heaven. A warmth overtakes my body and helps me doze off again.

This time, I dream of Clint graduating from high school and marrying a beautiful young woman, who I recognize but can't figure out the connection. If he's happy, I don't care about anything else. What a beautiful dream.

Chapter Twelve

I wake to someone or something banging on the exterior wall. I jump out of bed, ready to fight any intruder, dead or alive. No one — not even a rabid raccoon — wants to mess with me right now. Looking for a weapon, all I find is my solid mahogany jewelry box. Maybe it's an odd choice, but this sucker weighs a ton.

I bang on the wall twice to see if I get a reply—nothing. Drawing a deep breath, I open the window and look from one side to the next.

Fiddlesticks. No one is there.

Before I pull myself back into the room, I let the cool night air wash over me. It's refreshing, especially with these darned hot flashes that come and go these days. That is until a tingle crawls up my spine...too much of a good thing, I suppose.

Time to close this window and climb back in bed, or I'll never keep up with the boys tomorrow.

As I turn back toward my bed, I see a shadow out of the corner of my eye and drop the jewelry box, barely missing my still-healing foot. *Close one! What or who was that?*

I bend down to pick up the jewelry box and its contents that spilled across my bedroom floor. Earrings, necklaces, and bracelets are all wound up together, creating a puzzle rivaling a Rubik's cube. That's a problem for another day. I scoop up the mess and throw it into the box, ready to forget it until tomorrow, but something slides right through my fingers—the blasted prayer charm bracelet.

Do I dare check for a new message? I groan. *Who needs to sleep when there's a ghost on the loose?*

Ick. I don't want to open this tiny box of horrors, but I do it anyway. A skinny pink paper scroll falls out, and I pray—*God be with me and protect everyone in this loving home. Amen.* I never asked for any of this, but I know the good Lord is with me through all life's trials and tribulations.

Unrolling the scroll, I hold my breath. What message of doom and gloom does this note hold?

Your stalker revealed his face; go to the place of your youth. Use the keys you hold to open the gate; find the truth. Make the malevolent one pay. Don't forget to bring your new mate. Send the old one away.

My word—what a cryptic message! Why would anyone send this? Is this Carl's way of messing with me because he's jealous of my date with Brian? Not likely. He isn't clever enough to write a riddle. And knowing Carl, he would have pitched a fit in a much more dramatic way.

Regardless, there is no point in trying to go back to sleep. I may as well cook breakfast. The kids will be starving when they wake up.

I run down the steps to see Julia Caroline flipping fried eggs and pancakes on a sizzling griddle and tending to a skillet full of bacon. Bottles of orange juice and milk line the countertop, waiting for us to pour glassfuls for my sweet young'uns.

She looks up from the stove and winces. "I guess you didn't sleep a wink either."

"Nope—I'm plumb exhausted. Check this out. What do you make of it?" I hand her the pink scroll and share how my night went all cattywampus. Goosebumps pop up on my arms as I think of the evening's events.

"What? I don't get it, Nan. Who would send you a riddle from Other Side? Why not just come out and say exactly what you need to know? How is this helpful? "

"I suwannee—I surely don't know. I've been scratching my head over this since I read it."

Julia Caroline frowns. "Maybe it's your mama trying to send you a message. She was always a complex woman, and this is her bracelet. Who else knew about it?"

"Not a soul." *Could it be Mama?* I wouldn't have thought so. She hasn't made a peep since leaving this world fifteen years ago. In life, my family's matriarch was notorious for talking too much. I'd give anything to let her talk my ear off over a pitcher of sweet tea and some blackberry cobbler topped with homemade ice cream on the screened-in porch.

"Nan–I know what you're thinking. Don't get your hopes up that your mama will be able to spend time with you. Even if she's the one sending the messages, we don't know how often she'll communicate with you." Julia Caroline rubs my arm.

"But it could be her—"

Julia Caroline interrupts me. "I miss my mother, too. Life just isn't the same after you can't call up your mama to tell her about a bad day or share something really exciting. We've become the ones our kids and grandbabies turn to. I love you."

Wiping a tear from my eye, I clear my throat. "I love you, too. Right after Wesley and MaryAnne's accident, I wanted to call Mama more than anything in the world..." I trail off to catch my diminishing breath.

I adored my parents, and they loved Wesley and his family. If they were alive when the accident happened, it would have killed them. The fact that the boys need me is the only thing keeping me going.

"Maybe she heard my prayer and is trying to help us— wouldn't that be somethin'? She always knew just what to say to make me see things more clearly. When I got married, she tried to be supportive for a while, despite Carl's drinking habit. But she saw the bruises and told me to leave him. I finally listened when his fist landed me in the hospital."

Why did it take me so long to realize Mama was right? I could have spared Wesley and me a lot of pain.

Chapter Thirteen

As the sun lowers on the horizon, I decide to make a slew of biscuits for tomorrow's breakfast. While I load the second cookie sheet into the oven, someone knocks on the door. *Who could that be?*

"Just a minute!" I take off my apron, rub a bead of sweat off my forehead with my forearm, and shake the flour off my hands before answering the door. I bet I look horrendous right now. I turn to look in the mirror, but I trip over seemingly nothing. When I hit the floor, the door pops open to reveal Brian, holding a bouquet of calla lilies.

He throws the flowers on the ground and rushes to my side. Crouching, he grabs my hand. "Are you alright? Do you need to go to the hospital?"

Julia Caroline runs into the living room out of breath. "Goodness gracious! Whatever happened?"

My face reddens and I shake my head. "I was running to answer the door and tripped over my two left feet. I'm okay. Well … my pride may be a little bruised."

"Well, thank the good Lord!" Julia Caroline clutches her chest. "I thought we had another emergency on our hands."

"Another emergency?" Brian's eyes widen. "Is this a regular occurrence for you? Should I be worried? You do look rather pale tonight. Your skin usually has such a vibrant sun-kissed glow."

Julia Caroline squints and bursts into laughter. "You were making biscuits right before you answered the door, right?"

"Yeah. How did you know?"

She helps me to my feet and walks me over to the mirror over the fireplace. "Take a look at your...um...pale complexion."

Patches of white flour have ground their way into my normally rosy cheeks and chin. I look like someone who is dressing up as a mime or possibly a ghost for Halloween. No wonder Brian commented on my appearance. My stomach lurches. I certainly have a way of making an impression on people. It may not be a positive one, but a lasting impression, nonetheless.

Brian purses his lips as if he's trying not to laugh. He's too much of a gentleman to make fun of me.

The buzzer for the stove timer airs its annoying tone, and I groan. I'm not in any mood to continue baking, but my boys need a good square breakfast in the morning.

"Please excuse me. I'd better grab these biscuits, so they don't burn."

Julia Caroline waves her hand in the air. "Nonsense. You have company. Let me get them for you. As a matter of fact, I'll bring a couple out for you two to enjoy, and I'll get out of your hair. I'd say everyone deserves a treat after tonight's events."

When my best friend makes up her mind about something, she is impossible to dissuade. Julia Caroline is so sure Brian and I belong together. *Who am I to argue?*

She returns with a plate of biscuits, butter, and strawberry preserves, along with a pitcher of iced lemonade and two glasses. I ask her to join us, but she refuses. Instead, she places the tray on the coffee table and says goodnight.

"I don't want to be a third wheel. Y'all enjoy." She heads upstairs and turns back to smile broadly before going to the guest bedroom.

I gesture for Brian to take a seat on the sofa and sit next to him. For one time in my life, I am speechless. I never intended to date again. But I enjoy Brian's company. Shifting in my seat, I lean over to pour a glass of lemonade at the same time as him, and we bump heads. We both jump back in shock. Maybe I'm an unfit date this evening.

Just as I start to ask Brian to leave, he laughs uncontrollably. I can't help but stare. This has been a laughably awful evening. His infectious laughter makes me giggle, and I can't stop. Holding my abdomen, I suck in deep breaths and try to stop laughing.

Brian turns to face me. "At least I found out you're thick-skulled early in the relationship." He winks, and I melt. *Goodness —I really do like this man.*

I grin slyly. "And I love that you have a sense of humor. Life's too short not to have one."

His expression turns serious, and he leans closer toward me. My heart is pounding in my throat, just like a Palmetto bug bouncing on a trampoline. This is the moment. I draw closer to him, too, and our lips meet. He wraps his arms around me and pulls my body toward him. A familiar warmth surrounds us, and I don't want to let go.

I haven't felt this way since my honeymoon with Carl, right before the cracks in our relationship turned into canyons. Brian is different from Carl. He'd never hurt me.

After what felt like an eternity, Brian pulls away. His hazel eyes sparkle with a youthfulness. For just a moment, the fifty-two-year-old man I now know is replaced with the teenage boy I loved during our high school years.

He places his hand under my chin and locks eyes with me. "I should probably get going. Thank you for a wonderful evening. I look forward to many more. Goodnight, beautiful."

An uncontrollable shiver runs through my body as Brian leaves. I'm nervous and giddy at the same time. Not everyone my age gets a second chance at finding companionship and even more rarely...love. *Why did I avoid Brian's date invitation for months? When will I get to see him again?*

Julia Caroline walks into the room, wearing a smug smile.

"Why Nancy Parsons—you're positively sparkling. If I didn't know better, I'd think you've already fallen pretty dang hard for Brian. But you're not looking for romance, right?"

I slap her arm playfully and laugh. "I don't know what I need. Thank goodness you always do." *How does she have such a knack for it?*

"I'm so thrilled to be right in this case. You deserve to be happy!"

A blustery gust of wind barrels through the window, sending a chill down my spine. "Shut up! She does not!" A voice booms from outside an open window.

"Who said that?" I look out the window, but no one is there. The lights flicker, and I pivot toward the door. In the darkness, I see the profile of a man.

I gulp before I repeat my question, full well knowing the answer. The blood flowing through my veins turns icy cold.

How can I endure even a fleeting visit from my late, maniacal ex-husband?

"Looking for me?" Our unwanted visitor asks, sending my pulse racing. If I never saw Carl again, it would be too soon. Wesley's departure from this world makes his father's presence even more excruciating for me. Our son was the one good thing to come from our disastrous marriage.

Before I can muster the desire to face Carl, Julia Caroline beats me to the punch.

She stomps her foot, shaking the hand-scraped oak plank flooring beneath us. "What exactly do you think you're doing here? You're supposed to be on the Other Side. We don't have time for your nonsense. Now scat, you worthless beast!"

Drawing a deep breath, I pray Julia Caroline knows what she's doing and turn to see Carl's reaction to her command.

The apparition stands still, staring at Julia Caroline as if he is stunned. I know his silence won't last long. In life, the man never liked strong-willed women, especially my friends and family—the ones who insisted I deserved better than the likes of him.

I can't take it any longer. "Dang it, Carl. Why in Heaven's

name would you bother coming back to harass me? Wasn't it enough that you bruised my body and spirit when you were alive? You broke every promise you ever made me. You heard Julia Caroline—it's time for you to go back to wherever you've been the past fifteen years. No one needs you here."

He turns, locks eyes with me, and reveals a devilish grin. "I saw you with Brian. I thought you realized you could do better than that loser a long time ago. You married me instead—the smartest decision you've ever made. Besides, you wouldn't have had your precious Wesley without me. Speaking of which, I've seen our boy, skirting the in-between. It's time for you to come back with me, so we can be a family again. You know that's what is best. He'll never be able to rest while you're still here. Don't you want him to have peace? You belong with us."

I feel my jaw drop, but no words come out. *What can I say?* I would never choose to spend eternity with Carl, and I know beyond a shadow of a doubt I am Heaven-bound after I leave this world. I truly believe Wesley and MaryAnne will be there to greet me, but I don't want it to be anytime soon. I'm not done living, and five little boys need their nana.

Carl is obviously trying to antagonize me. And it's working. I've gotta to learn how to remain calm when I see him.

Julia Caroline steps forward again, lays her hand on my shoulder, and begins reciting an excerpt from the Bible's book of Psalms. "The Lord will keep you from all harm. He will watch over your life; the Lord will watch over your coming and going both now and forevermore."

A heaviness in the room lifts as Carl's spirit dissolves into an iridescent mist.

Chapter Fourteen

I've never been so relieved to see my ex-husband leave a room. In our dysfunctional relationship, that is saying something.

Julia Caroline cringes. "I despise that man more than the devil himself. I wish I could say that's the last we'll see of him, but we know that isn't true. We've got to crack the code that your messenger is sending through your charm bracelet. Let's worry less about who they are and focus more on what their messages mean."

I pull the scroll out of my pocket and read through it again.

"Your stalker revealed his face; go to the place of your youth. Use the keys you hold to open the gate; find the truth. Make the malevolent one pay. Don't forget to bring your new mate. Send the old one away."

Obviously, we know Carl is the stalker, and he just showed his ugly face here. But what does the rest mean? If I could figure out what the "truth" refers to, I might start unraveling the other pieces.

I scratch my head and stare off in the distance. "Wouldn't it be easier just to ask a priest to perform an exorcism on Carl?"

"There's no guarantee that will work. It can be very dangerous if things go wrong. Plus, we're not Catholic. Why would a priest want to help a couple of old Protestant women? I don't want to convert on behalf of Carl."

"Well, what about our pastor? Couldn't he help us?"

Julia Caroline massages the bridge of her nose. "He could bless the house, but your messenger's note indicates Carl isn't locked into this location. He seems to have free rein to haunt you wherever you go. I think protecting you is the answer."

"Go figure that son of a biscuit would follow me around now. I couldn't keep him at home—out of the bars and other people's beds when we were married." I spent so many nights lying awake, wondering where Carl was. The times I discovered his whereabouts, I often wished I hadn't.

Julia Caroline froze in her tracks. "Nan—you don't think the 'place of your youth' means Beaufort, do you?"

I gulp half a glass of sweet tea in one chug, pushing down the bile that threatens to erupt into my throat. It's been years since I've thought about my life with Carl in Beaufort.

Three weeks after our high school graduation, we got married in my parents' garden with only a handful of friends and family members as guests. That night, Carl announced he'd gotten a job in Beaufort as a deep-sea fisherman. Despite my protests, he convinced me to leave my beloved Isle of Palms, family, and Julia Caroline the following week.

I was too young to realize he wanted to get me out of my comfort zone and away from my support system. Beaufort, a mere two-hour drive, was far enough from our family and friends not to realize when our newly wedded bliss went South.

Everything seemed fine at first. Carl would go out with his crew for days at a time. I mostly kept to myself, tending to our cozy one-bedroom house on the marsh. When his ship came back to shore, we spent our days sunning and splashing at the little sandy beach along the riverfront and the evenings trying to start a family.

Those days spent together were beautiful. I didn't think my

life could get any better. However, I looked forward to becoming a mother, so I wouldn't be alone when Carl was at sea.

The babies didn't come as quickly as we expected. I often cried and wondered why. After trying for a while, Carl's attitude toward me changed. He would often slam things around, curse, and leave for hours at a time, coming back home drunker than Cooter Brown.

Soon, he started taking on more fishing trips with other crews, and I found myself not minding his absence. But I was lonely all the same.

As homesick as I felt, I couldn't bear telling my family and friends I'd made a mistake marrying Carl and moving away. When I called Mama and Julia Caroline, I pretended everything was okay.

After all, I had no reason to think he was cheating on me. He hadn't hit me...not yet.

To clear my mind during this tumultuous time, I often sat on our screened-in porch, watching the birds fly over the marsh grass and dip down to eat creek shrimp. Their grace and precision captivated me. Although marsh surrounds the backend of Isle of Palms, I hadn't spent days at a time on the Intracoastal Waterway. Having endless time to watch the wildlife made my misery more bearable.

After living in Beaufort for a year, I became numb to the sadness and desperation. One morning, I poured a cup of coffee and went out to the porch to watch the Sandhill Cranes perching on rocks. A loud bang reverberated throughout the marsh, and I searched frantically to find the source of the sound.

Stretching on my tiptoes and shielding my eyes, I saw a small red motorboat in the distance. The driver appeared to be alone. No one braved this section of the river because of the oyster beds, even at high tide.

Why did they think driving their boat through here was worth the risk? What produced the bang?

Did they shoot something or someone? I crouched behind the table on the porch but kept my eyes laser-focused on the boat.

As it approached, the driver's identity became clearer—a young woman close to my age. The boat appeared to be getting stuck every so often. Right in front of the porch, it came to a complete stop. The woman started yelling and smacking the dash.

I watched in horror and tried to remain concealed in my hiding spot. However, the woman made eye contact with me and called for help.

This was the moment I met Genieve Starling—a force to be reckoned with. Her flawless red lipstick, enormous white sunglasses, and green gingham sundress were only offset by a messy blond bob—clearly tussled during the wild boat trip. I soon found out she was trying to escape her daddy's wrath after she tried to run away and elope with a boy he didn't like.

After helping her free the boat, she promised to return the next day. True to her word, she showed up and came every day Carl worked. I quickly built a friendship with this woman who was unlike anyone I'd ever met—she painted her face, smoked cigarettes, and cussed like a sailor. But she was clever and knew the Sea Islands like no one else.

Genieve was a friend when I needed one the most. For the next nine months, we spent every day that Carl was away together. I was too young and naïve to know she would bring a whole slew of problems my way. *Boy, did she ever.* Rumors about her and Carl having an affair drove us out of Beaufort more than twenty years ago. Carl swore he hadn't even met her, but I didn't know what to think. I left without saying goodbye to Genieve, and I haven't spoken to her since.

A tugging on my pant leg brings me back from another time and place. I shake myself out of the trance.

Clint looks up at me with a wide smile. "Hey, Nana. Can I help you cook?"

My heart throbs. This sweet child always wants to help.

"Baby, you don't have to do anything. Go watch cartoons or play. I love you." I lean over and kiss the top of his head. He ran off, passing Julia Caroline on his way to the rec room. I didn't even realize she'd left the kitchen.

She places her hands on the butcher block countertop. "You alright? You zoned out. I made sure all the boys were up and dressed. The baby is still out like a light, but the other kids are watching a movie."

"What did I do to deserve you as my best friend? I'm so grateful for everything. I love you."

Julia Caroline wipes the corner of her eye. "I love you. We've been through a heck of a lot more than most married couples. We'll always be there for each other."

"Always, dearest! In sickness and in health." I wink at her and blew a kiss.

Julia Caroline laughs. "That's a vow we know we can keep! So, speaking of vows, were you thinking about living in Beaufort earlier and..."

"Genieve? Yeah. I'm afraid I may need to pay her a visit." Goosebumps prickle down my arms. I hug myself and try to keep the chills to a minimum.

"Are you sure that's a good idea? She brought you a heap of trouble when we were young."

"It's a terrible idea, but I think you're right about my messenger wanting me to go to the marsh. The rest of the message will make more sense when I'm there."

"I'll go home and pack a bag this afternoon so we can hit the road in the morning."

"What about the kids? I need someone they know to take care of them while I'm away, and if something horrible happens..."

"Don't say another word, Nancy Parsons! You don't want to borrow trouble. You're going to figure out this riddle and send Carl back to where he belongs. If you want me to come, just say the word. Susan and Jeremy are bringing their girls to town this weekend. The boys love their family. And you know that daughter of mine's motto: the more kids the merrier. If she hadn't started her boutique last year, she probably would have three more girls to raise."

"Let's hope it doesn't come to that. I just want to figure out what Genieve knows."

"Well...unless you're hiding a different 'new mate,' at some point you're going to need Brian to join you in Beaufort. You can call me when you're ready for us."

My head falls back. "Oh, my lands. I didn't think about telling Brian what is happening. How could I even start that conversation?"

"I'll figure something out."

Chapter Fifteen

The next day, I slip on a sleeveless dress, double-check my bags, and make sure all the boys have plenty to eat. After breakfast, I kiss each of them on the forehead and take Clint aside.

"Sweetheart, I'm going away for a few days. Julia Caroline is going to take great care of you and your brothers. Her girls are coming to visit this weekend, so you'll get to play with them. I promise I'll call you every day. I love you."

He fidgets for a minute but finally hugs my waist. "Love ya, Nana. I'm going to miss you." I pull him closer and suck back the tears that threaten to spill onto my cheeks. It's too soon to leave the children, even with my best friend who loves them dearly. But I remind myself I'm going on this trip to protect all of us from Carl—a thought I didn't expect on our wedding day.

I load my suitcase and overnight bag into the car and look back at the house one more time. Despite the tragedy we've faced, the home still radiates kindness and warmth. I'm grateful my boys have such a peaceful place to grow up.

Climbing into the driver's seat, I frown—this isn't the vacation of my dreams. I want to take the boys on a road trip to unwind sometime soon. Lord knows we all need it.

Seeing Genieve will be anything but relaxing, but if anyone has the answers to the riddle, it will be her. I hope she feels agreeable after so many years have passed since we last talked. I hadn't planned to leave Beaufort without saying goodbye, but the circumstances we faced left us no choice. Carl saw to that.

I pull a book on tape out of my purse and slide it into the cassette player before backing out of the driveway.

Setting course for Beaufort, I lose myself in author Anne River Siddons' spooky, suspenseful words. The Lowcountry draws paranormal activity and writers whose stories deliver chills and thrills. Anne's books are some of the best.

Traffic is light...thank goodness...I don't enjoy driving long distances anymore, especially in heavy traffic. *But who does?*

The further South I travel, the lusher the canopy of Spanish moss grows, creating a dark, eerie tunnel with few houses and buildings along the roadside. Well, no wonder all of us South Carolinians are obsessed with spooky happenings and books—we live on a living, breathing horror movie set. I laugh to myself but make a mental note to share my observation with Julia Caroline later.

When Carl and I moved to Beaufort, I knew the area held even more mystique than famously haunted Charleston—quite the feat for a small town. However, I didn't fully appreciate how embedded these legends were in island history and everyday life. Genieve and her family were at the center of it all.

Driving toward downtown Beaufort, memories of the early years of my marriage flood back. I grip the steering wheel tight.

This beautiful town served as the backdrop for pain, deception, and bitterness. But I loved the peacefulness of the marsh and the quaintness of the historic district.

I feel something brush my shoulder. I look down but nothing is there. Then, something catches my eye in the rearview mirror. Carl's apparition sneers at me, glowing an iridescent silver. My knuckles turn white, and I try to steady my breathing despite my racing heart.

"You came back, Sugar. We were young and full of passion. You were so beautiful. You still are. Just drive off the bridge, and we can be together again."

I let out a guttural scream. "I don't want a blasted thing to do with you. If you recall, we left Beaufort because of what you did."

He runs his icy hand along the outline of my face, wearing a nonchalant expression. Then, he presses his palm against my neck, making it difficult to breathe. I can't die like this. My boys need me, and I love them too much to abandon them. I focus on breathing through my nose as steadily as I can despite his firm grip on my neck.

I swerve into a shopping center parking lot and pull Carl's frigid fingers from my skin. "You will leave this instant and never return, not here, not on Isle of Palms, not in Charleston, not anywhere. I don't want anything to do with you. Do you hear me?"

Carl frowns and narrows his eyes and stares deeply into mine. "Bye for now, my love. I'll never give up on making you mine again. I'll take you with me next time."

His luminance fades until only the intense coldness remains.

I slam the steering wheel with the heel of my hand and try not to curse. Julia Caroline started a cuss jar for me, now that I have children living with me again. But the jar and the children aren't here. I feel like this is worthy of an exception. But I refrain. I've come to Beaufort to figure out how to deal with Carl. I just have to find Genieve.

What if she doesn't live in the same house or even in Beaufort? Oh lordy, what if she isn't alive? A chill tingles down my spine. I hadn't even considered how much Genieve's life had changed since I left town.

I've come this far. All I can do is try going to her family homestead. Hopefully, someone can point me in the right direction.

Around a bend in the road, I see the foreboding ruins of the St. Helena Episcopal Church Chapel of Ease—a place of worship for colonial planters who lived in remote areas too far from town to attend church services in Beaufort. The chapel burnt in the late 1800s, leaving a skeleton of the oyster shell tabby and brick structure. Along with its demise, came the ghost stories and local lore.

I'm tempted to stop and explore the ruins, as they've always captivated me, but I need to find Genieve first. As apprehensive as I am about our reunion, I know I'll be lost without her.

If I weren't a Christian, I'd swear I was in hell right now. But I know better, and I have an incredible amount of faith in God. He will watch over my boys and me. Carl won't win—he's on the wrong side of this fight.

After driving several minutes longer, the roadway darkens even more, and I come to the grand avenue of oaks that leads to Coffin Point Plantation. I crane my neck to soak up the view. The grand white house sits just past the intertwined branches, and it takes my breath away just like it did the first time I saw it.

Instead of turning there, I turn around and drive down the dirt road right before the avenue. My car scuttles down the pitted road, nearly bottoming out on a pothole and taking my disagreeable stomach with it.

Soon, I see the exquisite but smaller white home where I spent many lonely afternoons seeking the distraction I needed while Carl worked.

Gulping. I park in the driveway and walk up to the front porch. My stomach sinks. *Did I make the wrong decision coming here after so many decades have passed?* Perhaps I should have called first. I start to go back to my car, but I'm here. It's too late to turn back now.

While I'm debating ringing the doorbell or knocking, I hear footsteps approaching the door. Well, I'm going to look stupid standing out here, talking to myself.

The wooden door swings open, revealing a young woman—the spitting image of Genieve, right down to the red lipstick and snarky expression. I must be on the right track.

She props open the storm door and crosses her arms. "Yes?" *My...what a warm welcome!*

I force a smile. "I'm here to see Genieve Starling, or that was her maiden name at least. Does she still live here?"

The young woman's green eyes grow as big as saucers while she pushes her way out of the house onto the porch and closes both doors behind her.

"Who are you? And exactly what do you want from my mama?"

How can I answer? This girl is clearly trying to protect her mother. *Did Genieve have people chasing her down?* Not overly surprising—probably someone's wife. I'd hoped she'd outgrown her wily ways. Perhaps she hasn't.

I clear my throat. "Dear, I used to live in Beaufort, and Genieve and I were good friends. Can you tell me how I can find her? Does she still live here?"

The young woman buries her face in her palms. "Mama isn't doing well. She's on her deathbed upstairs. It's been a while since anyone other than Daddy has visited her. Can I get your name and see if she feels like having a guest?"

I nod and introduce myself properly. When the door closes behind her, my heart sinks. Genieve wasn't doing anything wrong. *How could I entertain negative thoughts about a dying woman?* She was a handful in her youth, but people change.

I came to Beaufort to get a handle on my life. I'm going to forgive myself and try to give Genieve the same grace once and for all.

Chapter Sixteen

Moments later, the young woman returns to the porch and leads me inside the rambling home. Polished oak floors and bright white walls provide a neutral but warm setting for understated furnishings. I'm surprised by the simplicity of the décor based on Genieve's bold outward appearance during our youth.

"May I get you something to drink... some pink lemonade or a glass of sweet tea?"

"No, thank you. I'd just like to see your mama if she's up to it."

The young woman nods and leads me up a winding staircase to a large bedroom with an abundance of sunlight pouring in from a side window. The scent of lavender fills my lungs, and I can't help but be enchanted by this beautiful room, similar to the way Genieve captured my attention the first time I met her.

Tucked in the shadowed corner, a thin woman with graying hair lies on a plush four-poster mahogany bed fit for a queen. The young woman helps her sit upright, propping her up with a stack of bed pillows and blankets.

We lock eyes and start to speak at the same time. I laugh and motion for her to begin.

She smiles a thin-lipped grin. "Nancy Parsons—you're the last person I expected to see around these parts," she said, drawing a ragged breath. "Although, I always wished you would come back to Beaufort without that dreadful husband of yours. Wait...he isn't with you...is he?"

"Well, in body, no." I pause. "But in spirit, unfortunately, he shows up at the darnedest times. That's why I'm here. I'm hoping you can help me figure out a few things."

Genieve nods, and I catch her up on everything that has happened since I left Beaufort. Her jaw drops when I talk about the years of abuse I suffered, the divorce, Carl's death, and my current predicament. I thought nothing would surprise her, but it just goes to show how extreme recent events have been. No one could make up nonsense this ridiculous.

Shifting in the bed, Genieve grabs an oxygen mask and places it over her mouth and nose. She closes her eyes and inhales deeply. *Should I ask her what is wrong? Is she going to recover?* It's none of my business, but I can't help but wonder.

As if to read my mind, she removes the mask and starts sharing bits of her life. "Remember, Bobby, the boy my daddy didn't want me to elope with? Shortly after you left Beaufort, we married and had our sweet Jane, who you just met. Isn't she lovely? She's taken great care of me since I got sick...lung cancer. I quit smoking years ago, but I guess it didn't matter. The damage was done. My lungs went on strike all the same. Now, the doctors say it could be two years, or it could be less."

I shake my head. "Life has a way of kicking all our butts. Everyone's time comes due. But that doesn't mean it's fair or we have to like it."

Genieve waves her hand. "I've lived my life to the fullest. When I was younger, I did a few questionable things, but I have no regrets. Why worry about things I can't change? God gave me my lovely Jane, and I've had Bobby in my life for almost thirty years. Not too many people get to experience that much love in their lives. I'm grateful for every minute."

I nod. Her way of thinking makes sense but is it okay to be so blasé about nearly ending someone's marriage—and that's only what she did to Carl and me?

God only knows who else Genieve's bizarre shenanigans harmed...intentionally or not.

Pointing this out right now would cause more trouble than it's worth. I need Genieve's help. If she gets stressed out, she might not feel up to solving my riddle. Guilt pangs rumble through my stomach, but I must protect my little boys. This is about them, not me.

Genieve coughs. "You're being awfully quiet. What are you thinking about?"

"I'm trying to figure out the next steps to sending Carl over to his final destination for good now that I'm here. Julia Caroline and I knew Beaufort had to be the 'place of my youth' the riddle mentions. But we're not sure why I needed to come here. We thought you could be the missing piece of the puzzle. Do you know what the 'keys' and the 'gate' might be? I've racked my brain over this part for weeks now, and I can't make heads nor tails of it."

"Do you have the bracelet with you? May I see it?"

I open my purse and pretend to look for it, even though I know for a fact it's inside the hidden zippered pocket. Do I really trust Genieve with this message transmitter to the Other Side? Hmm—not yet—maybe tomorrow. She seems harmless now, but you never know.

"Oh, dear." I frown and sigh. "I must have left it back at the hotel. I'll bring it back with me next time I come to visit."

Genieve's eyes widen. "You can't stay at a hotel! Please go pick up your things and stay here. We would love to have you stay with us. There's no need to pay for a room. Really. You're more than welcome."

I try not to make a face. "Thank you. I appreciate the offer, but I couldn't impose." There is no way on God's green earth I would sleep in Genieve's house.

"Well, the offer stands if you change your mind. I'll try to think about the riddle. Maybe something will come to me. Be sure to check the bracelet for other messages or clues tonight. My granny had a charm like that, but she wore it on a thick chain around her neck for safekeeping. She had some mighty vengeful spirits that she had to tend to."

I shiver. Genieve's granny was the real deal when it came to dealing with paranormal matters. I'm sure some people called her a witch back then, but when you live in a hotbed for stray ghosts, you'd best be prepared for anything.

Seeing Genieve's eyes droop, I realize it's time to leave. I thank her and say goodbye.

When I reach my car, I pull the bracelet out of my purse and open the charm. Sure enough, a pink piece of paper rests inside. My heart pounds uncontrollably as I unfold the note:

You're on the right track—stay the course. Don't let the vixen hold the key. The gate aligns where the flowing waters meet the green.

Great—another cryptic message—albeit a slightly clearer one. My messenger must have the same gut feeling about Genieve, the "vixen." *And the bracelet is the "key?"* I'm glad I didn't hand it over to her.

Those clues help, but there's no shortage of water or greenery in Beaufort. *How am I going to narrow down "where the gate aligns?"* Genieve probably knows, but I have to be careful how I broach the subject. She can't get ahold of the bracelet.

When I start to back out of the sand driveway, a loud clunk comes from underneath the car. I groan. *What the heck did I hit?* I hope I don't have a flat; I don't want to be here another minute longer than necessary. I climb out of the car and find a massive tree branch in front of my car. Thankfully, the tires are fine.

The sensation of someone staring washes over me, and I can't help to turn back toward the house. I slowly move my eyes upward to see Genieve watching me from her bedroom window. *I thought she was too weak to walk!*

I try not to scream at her. Instead, I jump back into the car, shift into reverse, and speed out of the driveway. When I look in the rearview mirror, I see someone standing next to Genieve. I squint—can't see their face. It must be Bobby, even though I got the feeling he wasn't home, based on what Jane and Genieve said earlier. I guess I was wrong.

When I come to the end of the drive, I look over my shoulder. The man wraps his other arm around Genieve's neck as if he is embracing her from behind. I can't help but notice the red watchband on his wrist. There's something familiar about it, but I can't remember why.

Chapter Seventeen

I've never been so glad to check into a hotel room as I am right now. A long bubble bath, followed by dinner and a glass of wine is in order.

Soaking in the tub, I think through the day's strange events. I knew this trip wouldn't be boring, and boy was I right. *What is Genieve not sharing, other than possibly not being as sick as she and Jane claimed? Why lie about such a thing? Did she want me to let my defenses down?*

Too bad, Genieve, I've got my guard up tenfold. You'll have to do better than that!

After bathing, I dry off and put on a clean dress and my single strand of pearls. Before dinner, I'd better call Julia Caroline and Clint like I promised. I love that kid something fierce.

I take out my long-distance calling card to cover the charges for calling Wesley and MaryAnne's house—I will forever think of it as their home, not mine.

As the phone rings, I hope Julia Caroline and the boys are home. I can't imagine her leaving with all of them in tow. If Susan and Jeremy had arrived, they might have taken the kids to the beach or out for ice cream.

On the third ring, Julia Caroline picks up. After asking about the boys, I update her on my conversation with Genieve and the recent note from my messenger.

"Nan - you don't know of anywhere the water flows through trees, or what about cypress trees? They grow in rivers near swamps and marshes. That may give you a starting point, although, I do understand what you're saying about the Sea Islands being eaten up with trees and waterways. That is definitely a conundrum. Whatever you do, be careful, hon."

"Don't worry. I will be, and I'll call you tomorrow around the same time. Can I talk to Clint?"

I hear muffled voices and a loud bang, like an avalanche of toys hitting the hardwood floors.

"Nana, when are you coming home? These wild boys are too much to handle. I'm ready to get my own bachelor pad and a dog. You can come and stay with me on the weekends. I'll make you spaghetti and cheesecake for dessert."

I stifle a giggle. "Honey, I should be home in a few days. Thank you for helping Julia Caroline while I'm gone, but you be sure to play with your action figures and have fun, too. Okay?"

"Yes, ma'am. I miss you bunches."

"Sweetie, I miss you and your brothers, too. But guess what— Julia Caroline's granddaughters will be there soon, and you can play with them. Isn't that exciting?"

"Yeah, except that Blake has been asking me to marry her every time they visit. I don't think that's what I want out of life right now. I need some space to figure out what I want."

Where does this child come up with these zingers? I cough to cover my laughing. "Well, there's no rush. Just go be a good boy, and clean up for supper, okay? I love you, and I'll talk to you tomorrow."

We say goodbye, and I can't wipe the smile off my face. Talking to that charming boy is exactly what the doctor ordered after having such an emotionally taxing day.

I check my hair in the mirror before I leave the hotel for dinner. The humidity has done a number on it, so I run a brush through my unruly locks and spritz a little hairspray to help hold my style in place. A smidge of peach rouge and mauve lipstick wouldn't hurt either. My pale complexion needs all the help it can get.

I'm not trying to impress anyone, but I'll feel better about myself. After applying the makeup, I take in my reflection—not bad for a quick fix on an old biddy.

Leaving the hotel, I walk toward the waterfront and settle on a restaurant with a patio overlooking the river. An osprey lands on the nearby bridge, and I can see its nest resting on a crossbeam. The only sounds I hear are boats on the water and the occasional family's chatter as they enjoy an after-dinner stroll.

This is the quietest meal I've had since moving into Wesley and MaryAnne's house. In some ways, I'm enjoying the peacefulness and solitude. I can rarely entertain thoughts that don't pertain to the children. At the same time, it feels wrong not to have the boys with me. But I remind myself they are safer with Julia Caroline.

This isn't a family-friendly trip in the least. Things will probably get worse with Genieve before they get better. She's a chaos creator.

When the waitress stops by to offer me dessert, I ask for a piece of peach pie to take back to my hotel room and for the check. She returns with a doggie bag packed to the brim with pie and tells me someone already paid my bill. I ask her who took care of my check, but she walks away without answering.

How strange! But after the day I've had, what did I expect — a completely normal dinner? Fat chance. I shrug off the weirdness and start walking back to the hotel. The display window of a small costume jewelry store catches my eye, and I go in to browse.

A rusty spinning rack filled with bracelets and pendants has seen better days, but I find a few noteworthy pieces.

The shop clerk wraps up my finds and locks the door behind me. It's getting late, I guess. I hadn't paid much attention to time. As I walk back to the hotel, the scent of the pie tempts me. I can hardly wait to dig in once I'm back in my room.

Antique streetlamps light the sidewalks, and a gentle breeze blows the draping foliage. I remember spending one of the few romantic evenings with Carl here, probably the night I conceived Wesley. We'd spent the afternoon strolling the waterfront, followed by a candlelit dinner where we talked about our future, which I now know was nothing but empty promises.

I soon realized Carl was more interested in womanizing anything wearing a skirt. When I asked him why he never came home anymore, he talked to me like the dirt beneath his shoes, and occasionally, punched me until I begged for him to stop.

Getting away from him was the best thing I ever did for Wesley and me.

When I reach my room, the bedroom lamp is on, but I'm certain I never turned it on. Maybe someone from the hotel turned it on, but there are no other signs of a turndown service.

Someone knocks at the door, and I open it to find the maid, asking if I'd like her to turn down my bed.

"Miss, did you turn on my lamp earlier? I didn't turn it on before I left for dinner. I'm sure of it."

She shook her head. "No, and I'm the only one working tonight."

I grit my teeth. "Would you mind waiting here for just a moment? I want to make sure no one is hiding in the bathroom or closet." I hope to goodness no one is waiting for me there. *Who could it be, though?* Genieve couldn't make it here...assuming she is truly sick.

She winces, but then, shrugs. "Sure. I'll take care of all my other housekeeping chores while I'm here. Let me know when you're done."

The girl obviously thinks I'm nuts. Hopefully, she'll call the police if I find someone hiding. I throw open the closet door... nothing there other than my overnight bag. Then, I walk into the bathroom. Holding my breath, I push the shower curtain aside.

No one and nothing to be found. *Why am I on such high alert?*

Walking back into the bedroom, I throw my hands in the air.

"No one is in here, of course. I've just had a long day. Thanks for your help." I retrieve a couple of dollars from my purse and tip the maid.

How embarrassing—I'm the hysterical old woman now. I'm sure she'll tell her coworkers how paranoid I am. But I deserve to freak out after the day I've had.

When the maid leaves, I sit down on the springy bed and scream into a pillow. *Wasn't it enough that Carl destroyed my young adulthood?* Does he really have to ruin my middle-aged life, too? It's not like I'm asking for an extravagant life, just the best one I can provide for my boys.

If Carl left me alone, the grandkids and I could have a good life—one they deserve.

I look at the clock; 9 p.m. is too late to call Julia Caroline without waking the children. I'll have to wait until the morning to talk to her again.

An intense scent of peach fills the air, and I look around for the source. The doggie bag from the restaurant catches my eye, and my stomach growls. I laugh. After eating a massive plate of fried shrimp and okra, I should be anything but hungry. I've always been a sucker for peach pie or cobbler, especially my mama or granny's recipes.

The waitress was kind enough to slip in a plastic fork, so I could eat my dessert in a civilized way. Believe me, I would have scarfed it down anyway, but I would have been ashamed of myself afterward.

Digging in, I savor the first bite of the piece—if you could call it that. I've seen smaller pies than this enormous slab. The peaches burst with flavor, and the crust is so buttery. Oh, my goodness, this is the tastiest dessert I've had in ages. I take another bite and close my eyes as I savor it. The only thing that's missing is a scoop of homemade vanilla ice cream.

I really should save the rest for tomorrow. *Who am I kidding...I'm going to polish off this entire piece.*

A few short minutes later, I felt like a glutton: the fattest of gluttons. *Why did I let myself overeat?* My eyelids are drooping, and I know sleep is imminent. *Good.* Sleeping is the best way to recover from eating half a peach pie.

I lie down on the bed, and the mattress cradles me perfectly as I drift off into a dreamless sleep.

Chapter Eighteen

I wake to the sound of rushing water. *What is that?* In the pitch blackness, I can't see my hand in front of my face. I feel for my bedside table and lamp, but there isn't anything within arm's reach. I'm almost certain I'm not in my hotel room. *One way to know for sure.* I try to step down from the bed, but my leg hits the floor as soon as I roll over.

Feeling around more, I can tell I'm sitting on a mattress on the floor. *Where am I, and how did I get here?* I pull myself up and tiptoe until I bump into a wall. *What the heck?*

A light flickers and filters into the room through gaps around the door. I hold still and try not to panic. I'm in a house, but I don't recognize the room. One thing's for certain, though. *I know Genieve is behind my kidnapping. I can't fathom why she would bother.*

The doorknob squeaks as it turns. *Who is there?* My blood turns cold, and I gasp. I back up as the door opens.

Jane stands on the other side, wearing a pointed expression. "Before you say a single word—you brought this on yourself. Mama tried to get that bracelet before you left, but you lied to her. So, now we'll do this our way."

"Why do y'all want the bracelet? I don't understand. What can you possibly do with it?"

"Oh, you'll see very soon. Now, hush. The rest of the house is trying to sleep. I can't have you waking up Mama." She leaves the room, closing and locking the door behind her.

I want to scream and cuss, but I'm not ready to deal with Genieve yet. I need some time to create a game plan before I have to listen to her give a B.S. reason for kidnapping me.

What a selfish, vengeful diva! I'll make her pay for this!

Pacing the floor, I punch the air. My orphaned grandchildren are waiting for me at home. There's no choice but to persevere. *Why does Genieve want this darn bracelet so badly? Well, shoot. As soon as I get rid of my sorry ex-husband, she can have it.*

When morning comes, I'll insist that Genieve let me leave and start exploring the Lowcountry, looking for answers to the riddles, so I can move on with my life. *She can hock the bracelet, for all I care. It's brought Mama and me nothing but headaches.*

I sit down on the mattress, surrounded by darkness and somehow nod off. This time, I dream about the night I left Carl. He yelled at me in front of Wesley, who was twelve years old at the time. When Carl reared back his fist, Wesley lunged at him. Carl started to hit the child, but I jumped in between them. I took the beating and yelled for my loving son to run as fast as he could to Julia Caroline's house.

The police showed up a short time later. They took one look at my collection of bruises and asked me if I wanted to press charges. That night, I finally listened to my mother and sent my husband to jail to protect my child and myself. I'll never understand why it took me so long.

I never let Carl lay a hand on Wesley. It was bad enough that he tormented me, but I married him. Wesley didn't choose to be born into our dysfunctional marriage.

Thanks to the Charleston County Department of Justice and our family court lawyer, that worthless varmint didn't see our son again.

Wesley didn't have a positive male role model in his life, but he didn't let that hold him back. He became the youngest police chief in South Carolina at thirty-one years old. He made it a point to protect domestic violence victims and their children at all costs. I couldn't be prouder of how he stood up for vulnerable families.

Because of Wesley's dedication to his community, thousands of people who live in the Lowcountry have a better life. There's no better legacy for him to leave behind for his children.

Images of Wesley's college graduation from the University of South Carolina, swearing into office as the police chief, and many other moments flood my mind, ending with memories of the day he married his match—the lovely MaryAnne. *I'm so glad my son married someone who shared his compassion for people. And, boy, what a romance they had!*

I admit I was envious of what they had at times. My happiness with Carl was so short-lived that I never experienced that kind of love.

Maybe I could have it with Brian—it's too early to tell, but I can't forget the sweet kiss we shared. I was so focused on getting rid of a certain malevolent spirit that I forgot to call him before I left town. *Brian is a good guy. If our relationship is meant to be, it will work out.*

A burst of light fills the room, and I struggle to open my eyes. Through the blurriness, I see Jane bring a tray into the room.

She sits it on the mattress next to me and clicks her tongue. "So sorry to wake you. But Mama is ready to talk. Now, drink some water and eat your toast and eggs real quick. We don't want you passing out while we're out today."

I sit straight up. "We're going somewhere?" I stare at the young woman; grateful I don't have to beg to leave.

"Don't play dumb. You know where we're going. Like I said, Mama wants to leave, so hurry."

I'm not sure why Jane thinks I know our destination, but I don't argue with her as she leaves the room. Relief washes over me, knowing I'll be able to get out today.

The eggs and toast don't look appetizing, but Jane is right

about one thing—I'll need my strength while we're exploring. *Please, Lord, help me end this nightmare quickly, so I can go home and snuggle with the little loves of my life. Those adorable boys will always inspire me to do my best. They're my true love story.*

Chapter Nineteen

Jane returns with my suitcase. "Don't get any big ideas about running away or any other nonsense. I took out your razor and nail file, but I have an overly sensitive nose. I don't want to smell your body odor. Clean up and change into some clean clothes; there's the bathroom. Be quick about it, we're leaving in five minutes."

I splash water and soap on the most important parts and dry off before slipping on clean undergarments and clothing. There isn't time to primp, but I absolutely have to brush off the fur that grew on my teeth overnight.

Running my tongue along my teeth, I feel so much better. Now, I just need to pull my hair back into a bun.

Someone bangs on the door. "Hurry up! Geez—you've been in there close to fifteen minutes." I bite my cheek to avoid saying a curse word. Closing my eyes, I draw a deep breath and pray again. God has my back. Everything will be okay.

When I open the bathroom door, I see Genieve standing in the living room. It takes everything I have in me not to call her a liar and ask who in Hades she thinks she is.

Her people had a deep connection to the paranormal world,

but they weren't dishonest, kidnappers, or thieves. I don't understand why she is going down this dark path. If she'd just been honest about her intentions with the bracelet, I might have been more willing to let her see it.

May as well get on with it. I move closer and clear my throat.

Genieve locks eyes with me, and I do my best to maintain a neutral expression when she speaks. "Nancy...I never wanted it to come to this. You have to understand—I didn't have a choice." She stops.

I can't hold my tongue. "What do you mean you didn't have a choice but to drug and kidnap me? How about earning my trust and asking for what you needed? That might have been an alternative." I stick my hand on my hip and tap my foot. I'm running out of patience.

Genieve wipes a tear from her eye. "I don't have much time. I'm trying to change that, though. I want to spend more time with Jane and meet her children whenever they come along. And I'm not ready to part with my true love."

Ugh. I almost feel sorry for her, but she's such a con artist. I don't know if I believe these theatrics. She's probably lying again.

Jane walks into the room and snaps her fingers. "Let's get out of here now. We've gotta leave before my husband gets home. He'll be fit to be tied if he finds out what we're up to." She grabs my shoulder and leads me out the front door and to a silver SUV. "Get into the vehicle and listen to me carefully. If you try to run away or make a scene, I'm packin'. I won't hesitate to shoot you dead and tell the entire world you attacked my ailin' mama. By the way, my uncle is the sheriff. He ain't gonna believe a word you say about us."

I don't want to show fear or too much emotion. Keeping my captors guessing about my plans and mental state is key.

They climb into the car, and I mask a sigh with a deep yawn. I hope exploring will take me to this mysterious spot where the "waters align with the green," so I can send Carl to his final resting place, and I can run away.

Jane pulls onto the main road; a chill fills the air. That's never a good sign in the tropical Lowcountry. Either something paranormal is afoot or an even more frightening and unlikely possibility—cold weather has found its way to South Carolina. I rub my arms, calming the goosebumps that prickle up and down my skin.

At the entrance to the Coffin Point Cemetery, the low-hanging Spanish moss whips in the wind at a fierce pace, never a settling sight in a place of rest, especially one that is nearly three centuries old.

Throughout the grounds, gravestones cast shadows against the patchwork of sand, shell, and grass. Epigraphs pull at my heartstrings, and I try not to let my emotions spiral as I read the inscription for a young man who died at the same age as Wesley.

Being an empath is never easy, and I've been overly sensitive since the accident. It definitely makes sense that I've started seeing Carl's spirit.

Was he there all along but I wasn't open to seeing him?

Genieve pulls out the scrolls from my messenger and the bracelet Jane stole from my hotel room out of her purse. "What is the riddle referring to? Is it a place that was special to you when you were younger? Why would anyone write messages in code like this?"

I shrug, but I'm beginning to understand my messenger's motives. They must have known the bracelet, or their messages might fall into the wrong hands. *How right they were!*

Jane grabs ahold of my collar. "We know you're hiding somethin'. Don't forget what I said earlier. I might look dainty in my sundress, but I'm packin' heat, and I'm a sure shot. Now, fess up about what you know."

"All I know is these messages started coming through the bracelet. I knew Beaufort had to be the 'place of my youth.' I haven't spent much time anywhere else outside of Charleston County. Once I figured that out, I thought your mama might have the rest of the answers. If y'all don't, though, we can call bygones, and I'll be on my way."

Genieve's jaw drops, and I start to walk away. Jane grabs me by the hair, puts me into a headlock, and presses her pistol into my back. "I said I ain't playing around. Now flippin' tell us what we're asking."

I bite down as hard as I can on Jane's arm, and she screams as she drops the gun. I kick the pistol into a nearby storm drain and smirk. "Guess we're on equal footing now, aren't we, sugar? Now, I want to hear from your mama exactly why she wants me to solve this riddle. How is it going to help her?"

Jane scowls, rubs the red marks left by my teeth, and I snicker. She shouldn't have messed with me. "Mama, you may as well tell her. What do you have to lose?"

Genieve wipes a bead of sweat from her brow with a shaking hand. "Not all of us had the perfect little life waiting for us on Isle of Palms. I had to stay back here and deal with the consequences of everything that went down when you left. Daddy threatened to send me to live with his sister on a farm in Wyoming when he found out I was pregnant. He made Bobby marry me, saying I was a slut and would be lucky if he would still have me. Mama stopped talking to me, and Granny cut me out of her will. No matter what I told them, they were sure Carl was Jane's father."

I stare at her. "So, what if they didn't believe you when you said you didn't sleep with Carl? You told me you made up the story as a prank to get them to let you marry Bobby. You got your way. What does that have to do with my bracelet and the messages?"

"It doesn't...not exactly. Let's just say I need the messages to connect to the Other Side just as much as you do, maybe more. They might save my life and help me find happiness with my true love."

"If I agree to help you, will you stop hurting me? Can we call a truce?"

"Truce...I swear on the Bible." Genieve holds up her hand. "You should know, I don't lie when it comes to Jesus, my family, or Chanel lipstick."

I bite my tongue and try not to laugh. I must have missed the Sunday school lesson about kidnapping being okay. "And what about her?" I gesture toward Jane. "Do you promise to try to stop killing me?"

"I guess," she mumbles and curses under her breath.

"Well, just know if you don't...the next time I bite you, I'll draw blood. I'm not afraid to go full vampire on your sorry butt. Karma will eventually catch up with you, young lady. I don't mind helping her get started sooner rather than later. Keep that in mind." I chomp the air and laugh uncontrollably.

Jane's eyes widen and she moves ten paces ahead of us. I laugh to myself—I'm glad I can scare bratty little twits like her.

Not being afraid to stand up for yourself is one of the greatest things about getting older.

Chapter Twenty

After walking around the cemetery without a sense of direction for another hour, I sit down on a wrought-iron and wood park bench. I don't understand what Genieve is looking for here; there isn't a body of water within a mile. *Do I dare ask her?*

I watch her and Jane wander, stopping to look at tombstones every so often and shake their heads. They continue walking in circles for the next half hour.

I'm beyond bored—it's time to move on to the next potential spot. They're wasting our time. *Could I make a run for it?* I can feel my heart throbbing in my throat, but I ignore it.

As I start to get the nerve to try, Genieve joins me on the bench. "Well, this is turning out to be a dud."

I scratch my head. "What are you hoping to find? I don't see what this place has to do with the riddle. Sure, there's a lot of green but not a drop of water to be found for over a mile."

She laughs and slaps my shoulder. "Nancy—you can't take things so literally. How do you propose we narrow down a place with greenery and water? Why you've described ninety percent of the Lowcountry. You know that as good as anyone."

"Of course I do, but I figured the riddle referred to a historically or paranormally significant place where these things come together."

"BINGO—where has more paranormal activity than a historic cemetery? The only trouble is we don't exactly have a shortage of old cemeteries and graveyards here in Beaufort, either. We just got to find the right one."

"How do you know what we're looking for?"

Genieve shook her head. "I don't yet, but I will when I see it."

Great...this wild goose chase is going to take longer than expected. I'm sure Julia Caroline wonders why I haven't called her in two days and will have a fit when she can't reach me at the hotel.

Jesus, be a fence and keep my best friend from killing Genieve. Julia Caroline is too pretty for prison. Besides, stripes sure won't go with her pearls.

I slap my hands against my lap. "Well, I think we should move on to a new spot. This one isn't turning up to be useful. But you did inspire an idea."

Jane mutters under her breath, and I flash my canines in her direction. She speed walks toward the car and gets in without saying a word. I smirk, proud of my victory. I know it's petty, but I don't care. I've spent my whole life trying to please others. It's someone else's turn.

Genieve and I get in the vehicle. I've never been so glad to feel air conditioning blow on my skin.

Using the rearview mirror, Jane looks back at us. "Mama, where should we go next?"

"I think we should try wherever Nancy is thinking. After all, it was her bracelet that has gotten us this far."

Jane stares blankly.

I grin as big as I can—*kill with kindness.* "Hon, please take us to the Chapel of Ease. It's the very definition of spooky and old. That place could scare the devil himself."

Genieve giggles but her expression turns more serious. "You're not wrong. The ruins are beautiful, but I've seen my share of things I can't explain there. My granny always told us not to go there after dark or even in the daytime, when the moon is full. I heard tall tales of all sorts of spirits who traipse those grounds day in and day out."

The only spirit I'm worried about seeing is Carl. But I suppose it will be necessary for him to be present to send him to his final resting place, assuming I figure out how to do that. *Hopefully, Genieve meant her promise of a truce.*

I don't have much choice but to trust her at this point. *I need her paranormal prowess to get me out of this pickle!*

Grand oak trees line the road, forming the mesmerizing, lush tunnel of Spanish moss that leads to the ruins. The foliage amplifies the dimness of dusk, creating a truly chilling scene. *Oh, wow— this is going to be creepy.*

When we reach the ruins, Jane parks the vehicle, and we get out to explore the towering roofless structure and grounds. With only the alabaster skeleton of the building remaining, there isn't much to take in from one end to the next. But it's the gravestones and tombs that we're here to examine.

Wandering, I read the names on the monuments—Fripp, Pope, Perry...nothing stands out as an obvious clue. *Dagnabit!* This place has to be the missing piece of the puzzle.

I can't bear another day away from my boys. *Something's gotta give.*

After we've walked around for a while, Jane turns to Genieve. "I thought this place was the answer to our prayers. I haven't seen anything interesting yet. So much for her theory. Big surprise."

I glare at Jane and start to deliver a dose of sweet-as-honey Southern snark, but Genieve shushes her. "Hold your horses, darlin'. We've been here less than an hour, and it's about to get dark. That's when things get interesting here. Be patient and give it a little more time. We may still find what we're looking for."

Lifting my head and hands, I pray aloud, "Lord, please reveal what we seek. Our safety, sanity and serenity are at stake. We need your guidance and support. Please give us a sign to get started. In Jesus' name. Amen."

Chapter Twenty-One

We make another thorough lap around the ruins, but nothing stands out as remarkable.

I purse my lips. "Sorry, y'all. Something in my gut told me this was the place. I guess I was wrong. Should we call it for the night and start again tomorrow? Maybe we should try the more literal approach and spend the day on the water looking for interesting greenery." *Ugh.*

Jane lets out an exaggerated grunt. *Great—she's mocking me now.* Flames appear in front of my eyes. I've made it clear I'm not a fan of hers. She's young but not naive. She should know better by now. I start to tell her off, but when I turn around, I see something else has garnered her attention.

A group of fireflies illuminate a small carving on a tree we must have walked past no less than a dozen times in the daylight.

Hmm...a tree is the literal definition of green. What makes this one special, though?

Does it hold the answers we need?

Genieve's eyes widen. "See! I told you this place comes alive after dark." I bite my lip, hoping she is right. It would be wonderful if we're finally making some progress in solving these impossible riddles.

We walk closer to examine the carving. It's a little hard to read the inscription, which is covered with debris. I pick up a stick and scrape off some of the moss and dirt. After putting a little elbow grease, I can make out the name *Robert Green. Is this the "green" from the riddle? It must be!*

My hands shake with excitement. *We're just one clue away.*

Jane pulls flashlights out of her bag and tosses one to each of us. We search for any reference to water on neighboring trees. The closest body of water is at least a mile away.

When we're about to give up, I trip over a rock and fall flat on my face. Goodness! I'm sure my cheeks are red, not that anyone can see them in the dark. I pull myself up and point the flashlight at the source of my embarrassment.

Holy cow!!! Etched into the rock are three snaking rivers that lead into a larger body of water. Of course, why didn't I think of it before—we're in the middle of the ACE River Basin, where the Ashepoo, Congaree, and Edisto rivers come together to form the St. Helena Sound. There's something magical about three powerful rivers combining forces in the beautiful sound.

Footsteps crunch the leaves behind me, and I jump, almost dropping my flashlight. Regaining my footing, I groan. "Who's there?"

"It's just me. I'm sorry I startled you," Genieve said.

I try not to roll my eyes. "Oh, what a relief—it's only my kidnappers."

"I know. I'm so sorry about this whole mess. We should have been honest and given you some time to get to know us. We don't know how long I have. If there's even a slight chance that I can get more time with my love, we need to do it while I'm still able to get out and about."

I sigh. I still don't trust them, but what can I do now? "Well, I wanted to work together to find answers. I guess we're both on the same page now."

"That's a relief. You've been over here for a while. Did you find something useful?"

I point to the rock and explain my theory. "I sure hope this is the answer."

Genieve pulls a bracelet out of her pocket, opens the square charm box, and stares inside. "Why isn't there anything in there? It always works for you. I don't understand. How do you do it?"

"You took that out of my purse? I don't know why I'm surprised." I shrug and shake my head. "There isn't always a message. I've only received two notes so far. I have no way of knowing when they'll show up. It's not exactly a scientific process."

Genieve hands over the bracelet. "Why don't you wear it? See if anything shows up while we're walking around."

I pull it around my wrist and close the lobster-style clasp. I purse my lips, trying not to laugh. They took my bait and stole the imposter bracelet I bought from the gift shop out of my purse.

I wince. "I've never worn it. I don't think that's going to help, but I'll give it a shot. Should go back to your house for the night and start again tomorrow? This has been a long day."

"No way! I feel better than I have in years. The fresh air has helped tremendously, and I finally feel like I have hope for the future."

I blow my hair out of my eyes. "Let's do it, then. Where do we go next?"

Genieve clasps her hands together. "I'm praying the bracelet will show us the way." It ain't gonna happen, not with this imposter bracelet and her poser prayers, but she can pray all she wants.

Headlights flood the parking lot beside the ruins. I immediately recognize the silhouette of the vehicle — Julia Caroline's classic Thunderbird. *Oh, goodness. Something scary is about to happen at the Chapel of Ease—only this time, it will involve the living instead of the dead.*

My best friend steps out of her car and places a hand on her hip. "Nancy Parsons, where in Sam Hill have you been? I've been worried sick about you and trying not to show it around your grandbabies. Poor little Clint asked me why you haven't called him the past two days."

I don't want to throw Genieve under the bus because we've finally reached an understanding, but Julia Caroline will see right through any lies I dish up. I can't even make eye contact with her.

Genieve clears her throat. "Hi, there. You must be Julia Caroline. I remember Nancy telling me so many marvelous stories about you. Please don't be mad at her. It's my fault. I've kept her wandering around these parts all hours, trying to find an answer to the riddles the bracelet keeps churning out. We need that sucker to spit out a new note. I know you've had some ghostly experiences. Do you have any ideas? Nancy—why don't you take it off and let Julia Caroline look at it?"

I unfasten the bracelet and hand it over to Julia Caroline, whose eyes widen as she opens the charm, and unsurprisingly, it's empty. I grit my teeth and try to force a smile.

She grabs me by the arm and turns to Genieve. "Please excuse us for a moment. I need to talk to Nancy about a problem with her grandkids real quick. We'll be right back."

After we're out of earshot, Julia Caroline furrows her brow. "What is going on? I know for a fact this isn't your mama's bracelet, which means you let Genieve believe it was for some reason. What really happened?"

"First, how are the kids? I've been dying inside worrying about them."

She nods. "They're doing great. Susan and Jeremy are taking them swimming tomorrow. They're pretty excited about being with the girls. Clint seemed especially happy when I told him I was coming to get you—we might be gone a few more days, but then, we'd be home. I also promised him we'd call tomorrow."

"Thank goodness! I'm breathing a little bit easier now, knowing my boys are safe and happy."

"Good." She nods toward Genieve. "Now, quick, spill the tea on all these shenanigans."

I fill her in on the events that have taken place to this point.

"Swear on your mama's grave you won't say anything about the kidnapping. Genieve and I are finally okay now. I even got her feral daughter to leave me alone. I just had to show her my feisty side."

Julia Caroline's jaw drops. "Are you okay?" I nod, but she insists on examining me to make sure I am unscathed. After a little bit, her shoulders relax, and she shakes her head. "I knew I shouldn't have let you come alone. Do you still have the real bracelet?"

"Yep. I have it put away for safekeeping. I can easily retrieve it when the time comes."

"Genieve had a point. Do you think you should check it for messages? Maybe it will point us to where we should go next.

"If I can look without those yahoos seeing me, it would be a good idea. I still don't trust them to have the actual bracelet. You know the 'key' the first riddle mentioned? I think it's the bracelet."

Julia Caroline's eyes lit up. "You're definitely on to something. I'll find a way to distract them."

Chapter Twenty-Two

Julia Caroline throws her car keys at me, runs back toward Genieve, and yells, "Goodness gracious. I think that bracelet's working its magic. It's making Nancy as sick as a dog. I think she just threw up a boot. You just give her a minute to rest, and I'm sure we'll have a message directly."

I grab a plastic Piggly Wiggly shopping bag and pretend to hurl inside. The sound effects and visuals must have been convincing. Genieve wrinkles her nose and turns away from the car. Jane is nowhere in sight, presumably disgusted by the thought of vomit.

How did Julia Caroline know an alleged puking was the ticket? She's so clever. I laugh to myself but take advantage of the distraction.

I pull off my left shoe and reach into my sock to retrieve the real bracelet from inside the cuff. I had no idea Genieve and Jane would kidnap me, but something told me they would try to steal the bracelet.

They'd never seen the real bracelet, and I knew the last place they'd look for it would be my sock. Turns out—I was right.

Holding the bracelet to my heart, I whisper a little prayer,

"Lord, please help us solve this strange mystery and send Carl on to his final resting place. We need your guidance through this perilous time. In Jesus' name. Amen."

As I open my eyes, the car shakes, and evil laughter fills the vehicle. Carl appears in his trademark silvery mist beside me. "Oh, baby. I've waited so long to make out with you in the backseat of this car. She's a beaut. What do ya say?" He wraps his icy arm around my neck and tries to pull me closer, but I push him away.

"I say, 'Get lost. You had your chance, and you destroyed my life. I refused to let you ruin Wesley's. That's why I left."

"Why are you always so hateful to me? You probably just need a good...scratch that...a great man back in your life to take care of you."

"I agree with you. That's the reason I started dating Brian again. He's the most honest, caring guy I've ever known. I shouldn't have ever broken up with him to date you. He is willing to give me a second chance. I intend to get it right this time."

Taken aback by my own words, I draw a deep breath. It may have taken an extreme life event to figure out how I feel about Brian, but better late than never.

Carl sneers. "I've been talking to Brian a lot lately. It's been a great reminder he isn't half the man I am. I'll prove it to you. Besides, I know for a fact he rode down here with Julia Caroline. I hitched a ride with them from Isle of Palms. They looked awfully darn cozy together in the front seat."

What? Carl has been talking to Brian—can Brian hear him? Brian is here? Why wasn't he with Julia Caroline? I'll have to ask her when I get a chance, but for now, I have to get rid of Carl even if it's just a temporary fix.

I clear my mind and recite Psalm 140:1 from the Bible:

"Keep me, Oh Lord, from the hands of the wicked; protect me from men of violence who plan to trip my feet. Oh Lord, I say unto you, "You are my God." Hear, Oh Lord, my cry for mercy. Let the heads of those who surround me be covered with trouble their lips have caused."

Making eye contact with Carl, I watch his apparition fade

until all that remains is a static-filled outline. Right now, he looks like our television screen when the darn rabbit ears stop picking up a signal during a storm.

It worked! Thank the Lord! The springy car seat squeaks as it bounces up and down during my victory dance.

Now, I can check the bracelet for a message. I open the charm and pull out a pale pink piece of paper. Holding the flashlight between my feet in the floorboard, I'm able to make out the message:

"You found the green, but you're a little off base about where it aligns with the waters. The Waters you seek have a head. Find their resting place and the rest will be revealed."

Waters must refer to a family's name. Of course, people have heads, but with the mention of "resting place," I'm guessing my messenger means a headstone. There isn't anyone with that name buried here or in the Coffin Point Cemetery.

I yawn and stretch. It's been an exhausting day, but at least I'm visiting some of the beautiful graveyards or cemeteries in Beaufort. Whether I like it or not, Genieve knows where the dead are buried across each square inch of the county. I still need her.

Groaning, I secure the bracelet in my sock again. Then, I get out of the car and walk over to the others to share the news.

Genieve claps. "Yes! I knew you'd be able to get the bracelet to work if you wore it. I'm sorry if that made you sick. It wouldn't be the strangest symptom I've seen from wearing a charmed object. Sometimes, the easiest option is the answer when it comes to this paranormal business. I know exactly where we need to go to find the Waters family's burial plot."

I don't correct Genieve. I'm quite content to let her think the new message came from the imposter bracelet.

Up until now, I hadn't considered the long-term importance of the bracelet to my family. It's the last thing of my mother's I still own, other than a few photos. I want to pass it on to my grandsons in case one of them has a daughter. I don't know how yet, but the messages have been crystal clear...we'll need it to send Carl away for good.

We walk back to the parking lot in silence. This is the first time in days Genieve and Jane aren't running their mouths. What are they up to?

When we reach the Thunderbird, I get in on the passenger side. Before I can close the door, Jane grabs the handle. "Where in the heck do you think you're going? You're riding with us."

Julia Caroline revs the engine. "Young lady, I'm getting ready to throw this baby into drive. You'd best let go of the door and hop into your own car. We'll follow you. Trust me, we didn't come this far to turn around and go home now."

Jane looks at me, and I nod. "Trust me. I would do what she says. She means business. You just thought I was mean." Julia Caroline cackles for a moment, and I grin.

We try our hardest to be nice, but when someone crosses our loved ones, watch out!

I lean my head out the open window and point at Jane. "You have my word—we'll be there. We gotta stop by the hotel to pick up someone. The first riddle referred to my "new mate." He's the closest thing I have."

Jane scowls but walks off and joins Genieve in their SUV. Julia Caroline follows them as we wind through the country roads toward downtown Beaufort.

"You saw Carl, didn't you?" Julia Caroline asks.

"How did you know?"

Julia Caroline bit her lip. "That's the only way you could know Brian came with me. Are you okay? Did the old hateful goat say anything useful?"

"I'm fine, and of course, Carl didn't have anything helpful to offer. He was just as possessive and crazy as he's always been. Speaking of unbalanced people, how did you know I need rescued from Genieve and where to find us?"

Julia Caroline smirks. "I've never trusted Genieve since the first time you talked about her, and I knew I needed to bring Brian to you, anyway. I didn't want to expose him to more super-natural weirdness than I had to, so I figured we'd wait until you had a set location to bring him into the picture. When you didn't call, I remembered you talking about this place and how spooky it is. I hoped I'd find you here."

"How did you convince Brian to come with you? Carl said something about talking to him, but it seems like Brian would have said something to me sooner. Did he freak out when you told him?" My chest sinks, imagining his reaction.

"At first, I told him you needed his help. He didn't ask any questions, just showed up with an overnight bag about half an hour later. But when we got into the car, he asked me if your problems related to Carl. When I nodded, he turned pale white and told me Carl has haunted him continuously for years, threatening to kill him if he tried to date you. Apparently, when Lorna died, Brian started seeing and communicating with spirits. Unfortunately, he got the short end of the stick with Carl being his most frequent flyer. Brian has been working up the nerve to tell you. He said he tried on your date, but the timing never worked out."

I can't believe it! I'd worried about telling Brian about Carl's haunting. Sounds like he'll be pretty understanding. I'm so glad I won't need to explain how everything works, not that I'm the expert.

As we reach the hotel, my shoulders tense. I'm not thrilled about introducing another romantic interest of mine to Genieve —since she was the beginning of the end for my marriage to Carl. No lady should ever try to seduce someone's husband.

Chapter Twenty-Three

After Brian joins us in the Thunderbird, we motion to Jane and Genieve that we are ready to move again. Julia Caroline follows them back to the main road, and we update Brian about the happenings to this point.

I sigh, staring out the passenger side window. "I wouldn't blame you if you left now. You don't have a stake in the game. You'd be smart to go home. This trip has been quite the disaster."

Brian leans forward from the backseat and places his hand on my shoulder. "I'd never do that to you. Don't you know you're the stake in the game for me? You always have been and always will be. I want to be here and to help you get rid of Carl so neither of us ever has to see that sorry SOB again."

Reaching up, I squeeze his hand. The warmth comforts me, but a lump forms in my throat. Is this what having a supportive partner feels like?

I've never been in an adult relationship with someone who cared about me more than himself. I push the lump down, avoiding the swirling emotions that try to surface. Now isn't the time to fall apart. I'll save that for when I'm back home and in the privacy of my bedroom.

Julia Caroline's eyes dart over toward us, and she smiles broadly. My best friend is so transparent, but I can't be mad at her. For the first time, I'm not annoyed by her matchmaking efforts. She's prayed for me to find someone worthy of my affection, even though I'd given up on the notion years ago.

Losing Wesley and MaryAnne reminded me how short and fragile life can be.

I have to set a good example for my boys, showing them we all deserve a companion who loves us for who we are and treats us with respect. When they grow up, I want them to find love and happiness.

Looking out the window again, I take in our surroundings. We've made it back to Coffin Point Plantation, but instead of heading toward the cemetery, Jane takes a sharp turn down a dirt and shell road. The Thunderbird rumbles behind, jostling me around. I'm sure I look like a popcorn kernel bouncing around an air popper. Let's hope my bladder doesn't pop.

When we reach a small shack beside the waterfront, Jane parks the SUV and Julia Caroline pulls beside her.

I get out of the Thunderbird and soak up the breathtaking, eerie scene. A massive oak tree towers over the crumbling house. Strands of Spanish moss whip in the breeze, beckoning us to come closer.

The sensation someone is staring at me creeps in, but the rest of our group is standing by the water. As I walk down to the bank, goosebumps pop up along my arms, and my teeth chatter, despite the balmy temperature and unrelenting humidity. Is Carl waiting to come out from his hiding spot and torment me? Probably. But hopefully, we're close to figuring out the remaining pieces of the puzzle to banish him to his final resting place.

Genieve holds a flashlight up toward her face. "Is everyone ready?" Each of us nods, and she continues, "The Waters family owned this house. They loved the St. Helena Sound and chose to live below their means just to be close to the water. When each family member passed, they were buried behind the house. I should have thought about them the first time you shared the riddle."

I shrug. "All we can do is guess. You couldn't have known the riddle was referring to a name, not a body of water. It was such a cryptic message. What comes next?"

Genieve motions for us to follow her, and my stomach churns. Can I really trust this woman—what if she is leading us to a trap? My shoulders tense. I asked her to help me. We're in too deep to leave.

Behind the shack, seven gravestones surround the base of the oak with others throughout the backyard. Despite the state of the house, someone has maintained the monuments right down to the fresh cut roses poking up out of vases built into each grave. The flowers couldn't have been there more than a day. Who would take the time to come all the way out here? Do they have family members who still live in the area?

I take out a flashlight and read the epitaphs. Samuel Waters, the eldest family member buried here, died in 1889, and his great-granddaughter, Marion, was buried in 1965. Wait—why did the riddle send us to the Chapel of Ease, and back to Coffin Point Plantation? What a wild goose chase!

Jane reaches into a tote bag, and her hand brushes the pearl handle of a revolver. I prepare to pummel this idiot. Did she really bring another gun with her? This is getting old. I brace myself for the worst.

She reveals the stone I tripped over at the ruins. "Glad I picked this thing up earlier."

I breathe a sigh of relief. "What are you going to do with that?"

She shrugs. "I'm not sure, but something told me it might be useful." Maybe she's smarter than I thought.

Brian yelps and falls to the ground. I run to his side and kneel to examine the foot he's clutching.

"What's happened? Did you break something?"

"I think I'll be okay. I twisted my dang ankle on somethin' over there." He points to Samuel's gravestone, and I run over there. A large intricately carved stone structure juts out of the ground behind the grave. I bend down to get a closer look and see a fist-sized hollow section in the stone. I gasp—Jane's stone may fit.

"Jane! Come here now!"

She runs over, and I show her the opening. "What do you think? Should we try it?"

Jane's eyes widen as she squats and places her stone inside the indentation. "No way! It fits!"

My blood pumps at the speed of light. *Who could have imagined this would work?* It's something straight out of Wesley's favorite Indiana Jones movie. Our messenger from the Other Side steered us in the right direction. *How did they know such things existed way out in the deep Lowcountry?*

Genieve runs over and claps. "Wow! My granny would have squealed like a pig to see this contraption. She always talked about finding hidden clues to the paranormal world, but I've never seen anything like it. Try twisting it clockwise to see if something else happens."

I close my eyes and pray for a miracle.

Chapter Twenty-Four

Jane rotates the smaller stone half an inch clockwise and stops. "It's jammed!" She struggles, trying to free it from the enclosure. After a few minutes, Jane throws her hands in the air. "I can't get it out. What are we going to do?"

I step closer and feel the worn indentations along the border of the smaller stone. Carved slash marks point counterclockwise, so I try moving the stone in that direction instead. It budges a hair, but not a significant amount. *Hmm...maybe we had too high of expectations for a rock.*

Leaning in closer, I notice something small and white is packed into the lower left crevice where the stones meet. I try brushing the object away, but it stays in place.

Reaching into the zippered pocket in my purse, I pull out a pair of tweezers and tug on the object. After digging for a bit, the smallest sand auger shell I've ever seen pops out of the hole. I shake my head. *You never know where you'll find these darn shells or clumps of sand in the Lowcountry.* I twist the stone again. This time, it moves with ease, grinding against the enclosure until it's made a full revolution.

Nothing happens. *How anticlimactic*! I try moving the stone again, but it's locked into place. *Well, poo!*

Genieve shakes her head. "That should have done the trick. What are we missing?" She runs her hand along the enclosure and winces. "I think there's another small notch here. It's round. What else could go in there?"

The charm from my bracelet! My stomach aches when Genieve stares at my wrist, clearly eyeing the prayer box. If I give her the imposter, it won't work. But as soon as I dig in my sock for my mother's bracelet, Genieve will know I've been lying. I feel like such a fraud even though I lied for the right reasons. All of that aside, I don't want her to have access to my heirloom or its connection to the spiritual world.

I shine my flashlight where Genieve pointed. Ugh...the charm would perfectly slide into that space. My stomach muscles contract as I try to think of an alternative. But there isn't one.

Julia Caroline locks eyes with me and shrugs. We've been friends long enough to read each other's minds. She's definitely telling me it's time to take a chance. As always, she's right.

I groan and bend over to pull the bracelet out of my sock, almost falling over. Why is balance one of the first things to go when you hit fifty?

Before I fully regain my footing, Genieve grabs the bracelet out of my hand. "Tsk. Tsk. Why did you pretend that trashy souvenir shop costume jewelry was your heirloom? Did you really think I wouldn't know the difference? No good Southern lady would wear jewelry that turns your skin green. I know your mama raised you better than that."

Jane moves closer again. "I have another gun. Just try somethin'. I'll shoot you and throw you to the gators in the marsh."

I smile widely and point to my teeth. "Girl, you just try it. Don't forget, I don't need no darn gator to do my chomping for me. I'll chew you up and turn you into fish food myself. Let me know when you want to start. I'll sharpen my teeth while I wait."

I turn to Genieve. "I thought I needed your help to solve this mystery, but I vastly undervalued my own know-how and strength. I'll never make that mistake again."

Julia Caroline's eyes glow, and she gives me two thumbs up. "You go, girl. Tell her how it is."

Genieve scowls. "Now that everyone has that out of their system, let's just see if the charm works."

I take the bracelet out of her hand. "It was my mama's bracelet. If anyone is going to do this, it should be me. Besides, it probably won't work for anyone else."

Julia Caroline points the flashlight toward the notch. "I gotcha covered. Go for it when you're ready."

As I pinch the charm clip to remove it from the bracelet, I draw a deep breath. *I sure hope putting the charm into the stone doesn't destroy it. We're in so deep now, though. There's no going back.*

I insert the charm inside the opening and step back. Air whooshes from around the charm, and a round stone door rolls in front of it. The entire enclosure presses inward, crunching loudly and spinning in a circle.

I grit my teeth. *That can't be good for the charm.* I hope I made the right choice.

The door rolls away, and my shoulders tense. I reach inside the notch to remove the charm. I'm afraid to look, but I may as well assess the damage, so we know what we're working with now.

The circumference of the charm hasn't changed. Lengthwise, it has stretched into a bullet-like shape. Running my finger along the sides, I feel a spring mechanism I never noticed. An ocean wave design swirls around the center of the charm. When I press the top and bottom together, it collapses back into its normal state.

I hold it up toward the flashlight. "Well, I'll be—where the green aligns with the waters. We've found it. Have you ever seen anything like this?"

Julia Caroline's eyes widen. "I don't reckon I have. What do we do next? Did you get another message?"

"Let's see." I open the charm clasp and find a pink piece of paper. While reading the note, I grit my teeth — "*Now, you under-stand the charm. Keep it away from those who mean you harm. Expand it to reveal the wave. Press it into the notch until it clicks, remove it, and when the angry one appears, be brave.*"

My hands tremble. Brian holds them tightly and kisses my cheek. "You're going to do great. And you have Julia Caroline and me here with you. Let's send Carl away for good." I nod and smile. Brian has quietly observed the shenanigans to this point, but it makes me feel better knowing I have him in my court.

Steadying my hands, I follow the instructions from the note.

Chapter Twenty-Five

The charm slides deeper into the notch, and I turn it counterclockwise until a whistle reverberates through the deep rocky channel. I stand back and stare at the enclosure as the charm spins back to the surface. This is the oddest thing I've ever experienced.

Genieve nudges me. "I think you should take it out now."

"Here goes." I retrieve the charm and open the latch. Another piece of pink paper waits inside. Opening the note, I hope it's the last one. We need a solution to end this madness. I'm ready to be home with my boys, all of us safe and sound.

Julia Caroline holds the light closer for me to read the note — *"You opened the portal and can send the evil one to the Other Side. Share reasons he should move on to his next life. Under the light of the full moon, replace the charm, turn it until the whistle sounds, kiss your new mate, and forget about your strife."*

"Oh, is that all we need to do?" I groan, but nothing is hopeless with God on our side. I bow my head and pray, "Please, Lord, let this work."

"Amen!" Julia Caroline nods enthusiastically. "I want you to be free from your beastly ex-husband once and for all. I'll never understand why he wants to torment you. Putting you through hell during his lifetime wasn't enough. He just had to continue torturing you from beyond the grave."

A breeze sends a chill down my spine, and the fuzzy outline of a specter forms. I don't want to see Carl, but, with any luck, this will be the last time. The fuzziness transforms into glistening iridescence.

Carl's trademark sneer comes into view, and I brace myself for whatever comes next.

"Hey, there, darlin'. I'm taking you back with me this time. Don't you want to be with our boy again? He's waiting for you."

"Shut up, Carl. Wesley would never talk to you. Even if he did, I'm staying here with his boys. You're dead. You need to leave all of us alone and go on to your final destination. Aren't you tired? Go rest and find your place of peace."

I hold my hand up toward Heaven and recite Ephesians 6:14-16 — *Stand firm then, with the belt of truth buckled around your waist, with the breastplate of righteousness in place, and with your feet fitted with the readiness that comes from the gospel of peace. In addition to all this, take up the shield of faith, with which you can extinguish all the flaming arrows of the evil one.*

Carl shrugs. "Why are you bringing the Bible into this? I don't need a Sunday School lesson right now."

Julia Caroline waves her hand. "Don't you worry your ugly little head about it, Carl. Why can't you just leave my girl alone? She's never needed you for anything. And that hasn't changed."

Carl shakes his finger at her. "There you go again, butting into our business. What else is new?"

Julia Caroline pulls out a silver cross pendant from under her blouse and held it toward him. He shields his eyes. This is why I love my best friend. She is intelligent and not afraid to take on anyone, especially when it comes to protecting people she loves.

She motions toward me. "Hurry! Put the charm inside the darn rock!"

I lean toward the enclosure and start to place the charm, but

Jane lunges toward me, knocking it out of my hand. Then, she tackles me to the ground.

Writhing underneath her, I try to bite every appendage within reach. I want to make good on my promise to draw blood this time. This girl needs to learn a lesson. Before I can inflict a puncture wound, Julia Caroline hops on Jane's back and pulls her wrists together, securing them with a belt.

What a scene! After I catch my breath, I rise to my knees and I look over at Brian, who is wearing a wide-eyed expression. I doubt he knew quite what he signed up for; none of us did.

Where is the charm? I point the flashlight where I thought it thudded, but it's nowhere to be found. My stomach aches. What will we do without it?

Genieve walks over and opens her palm to show us the charm. "Looking for this?"

"Thank goodness you found it! Now, I can finish what we started and give Carl a one-way ticket the Other Side."

She laughs. "I don't think so, but I truly appreciate your help uncovering all these clues for me." I scratch my head. Does she want the honors of sending him away?

I shrug. "If it makes you feel special to be the one to send him away, be my guest. I just want him to leave."

"Oh, sugar pie, you're not understanding. He's not going anywhere. We just needed your charm bracelet and the riddles from your messenger, so we could find the portal and seal it forever." She smiles broadly. "I knew whoever sent those messages would only communicate with you. We had to keep you alive until the very last moment. You probably should have taken the notes about not trusting me to heart. If I were you, I would have locked me up somewhere I couldn't escape."

I shake my head. "But you said you didn't even know Carl when we left Beaufort. You told me the rumors weren't true."

"You were so naïve back then. I could have convinced you the sky is green, and the grass is blue. You're not the same gullible girl you were then. Or are you? Don't you see the resemblance between Carl and Jane? Clearly, he is her father; you can't deny it. And he's the love of my life. I won't let you send him anywhere."

How am I supposed to react to his outburst? What little food I have in my body churns, and I ball my fists. *I should choke her, but I'm going to count to ten and try to chill out.*

I look over at Julia Caroline to make sure she has the other jerks under control. Jane is lying on the ground with her wrists bound, and Carl is cowering under Julia Caroline's pendant. I notice his watch—a red and black University of South Carolina Gamecocks band.

How could I have forgotten? When He bought that watch when Wesley was accepted into the university and sent us a picture to show his pride. Our son didn't fall for his too little, too late attempt at being a decent father. I realize this is the very watch band I saw on the man caressing Genieve as I left her house my first day in Beaufort. What a home-wrecking floozy!

I can't control myself. I slap Genieve across the face twice and let out a series of guttural screams. "You whore!"

Chapter Twenty-Six

Brian pulls me away from Genieve before I can beat her senseless. "You're better than this trash. She may be wealthy, but she is pure trash." He spits at her feet. "Don't let her distract you from what you're trying to do right now."

I nod and take a deep breath before turning to her. "Where is the charm? Give it to me now."

She rubs the red mark on her cheek and cries. "You had such a perfect little life—a cute house, a husband and a wonderful family back on Isle of Palms. No one ever loved me, not even my parents. Bobby only married me because he wanted a job at Daddy's law firm. We've always had separate bedrooms. I was jealous of you, but I never meant to have an affair with Carl."

I bite my lip to prevent screaming again. "What is that supposed to mean?"

"You were away one weekend visiting Julia Caroline. I didn't know you were gone when I dropped by your house. Carl invited me in, and we had a few drinks. Before I knew it, well, you know what happened. I felt horrible at first, but we started seeing each other more often and eventually fell in love. When all the rumors spread, Carl thought it would be best for y'all to leave town. It broke my heart, but he still made time to come see us. Now is our time to be together forever."

I shake my head. "Why did Carl come harass me, then? If you're so happy together, why even bother me? I wouldn't have known."

Genieve winces. "It's like I said — you were our ticket to getting the clues to unlock the portal. We want to make sure he can stay here forever. Can you help us seal it up? We'll never bother you again."

Julia Caroline motions for me to join her beside the rock enclosure. "I have the charm. It's a full moon. Now's the time if you're going to do this. These two aren't ever going to let you live a normal, peaceful life. You know Carl is such a narcissist that he doesn't want you to be happy with anyone else. I'd nip it in the bud right now."

She's right. I can't take a chance letting Carl roam the earth for a minute longer. Even if I wanted to be nice to Genieve for some bizarre reason, Carl's existence threatens the safety of my sweet babes.

I run over to the stone enclosure and grab the charm from Julia Caroline. I look over at Brian to make sure he's still game, and he nods. Whew! Thank goodness! I haven't had anyone else come close to becoming a mate in so long. He's key to following the riddle's instructions.

Here we go! I push the charm inside the notch and turn it until the whistle echoes. Brian leans in to kiss me, and a whirl-wind forms around us. We're almost levitating as airborne leaves swirl around our bodies.

Maybe it's a bit of magic, or it could be the first inklings of love, giving new meaning to being swept off your feet. Whatever propelled us off the ground, I could live in this moment forever.

Brian's embrace comforts me, and his lips spark electricity throughout my body. As we pull away from each other, I'm breathless.

Julia Caroline yells, "It's working!" She points at Carl's

wavering apparition. "C'mon, Nan! Recite another Bible verse and tell Carl to move along to his final resting place!"

I shake out my hands to release nervous energy. "Carl, go on to your final destination and leave this world behind forever. Dear Lord, although he means me harm, please have mercy on this man's soul. In first Corinthians, you say, '*Love does not delight in evil but rejoices with the truth. It always protects, always trusts, always hopes, always perseveres.*' I put my faith in you, Lord. Thy will be done."

The silvery outline around Carl melts into a static blob and drifts in a cloud of particles toward the opening in the stone structure.

Is this really the end? Am I finally free from this malevolent mother trucker?

Genieve wails, "No, my love! Take me with you—I won't ever be the same again." This is pathetic. I almost feel sorry for Genieve, but then, I think better of it. She's reaping what she has sown.

Carl's iridescent hand reaches out for her, and she grabs a hold of it. As he floats into the structure, she follows him inside, and the door thunders as it slams closed behind them. I can't imagine wanting to spend eternity with Carl. She said she was dying, but I have my doubts about the severity of her illness.

Are both of them really gone for good? Could I really be that lucky?

I shine the flashlight from the top to the bottom of the structure. The notch and the enclosure have vanished. Only the smooth flat stone surface remains.

Where did my mama's charm go? I get on my hands and knees, searching for the shiny silver contraption. Never in my wildest dreams did I expect what happened tonight, nor that the charm would transform and disappear. My heart aches.

Julia Caroline joins me in my search, but after a few minutes she stops me. "I had a feeling it would travel along with Carl, but isn't it worth the cost to be free from him?"

"Of course, but that doesn't mean I won't miss one of my last links to my mama. What if she was the one sending me the messages? I'll never hear from her again. Doesn't that beat all?" I hug myself, trying to soothe my nerves.

Julia Caroline gestures toward Jane's SUV where the young woman is bawling her eyes out. "It looks like someone else is missing her mama right now. Maybe you should go reassure her she'll be okay. You don't owe Jane anything after what she and Genieve put you through, but it would be the Christian thing to do."

I suck in a deep breath. "Why are you always so dern right about everything?"

I don't wait for an answer before walking over to the SUV. I knock on the window, half expecting her to come out ready for a fight. Instead, she opens the door and throws herself on the ground.

Brian helps her back up into her vehicle, and my motherly instincts kick in. I have to hug her. As much as I might despise this girl, I can't let someone suffer. That's how I was raised, how I raised Wesley, and how I'll raise my grandchildren. Compassion and empathy are everything.

Between sobs, she squeaks out her thoughts. "Mama's life was harder and more complicated than I ever understood. I thought Daddy...er Bobby...was my father until last year, when I saw Carl's spirit wandering around. He told me the truth, and Mama fessed up. I'd only seen my granny's ghost until that point. Mama had tried to protect me from the paranormal world, saying it only ended in heartache. Now, I understand what she meant. I'm absolutely crushed."

"Bless your heart. What a horrible realization for a young person. I'm sorry you had to go through this. Do you want us to take you home? Bobby or your husband can help you get your car later."

Jane shakes her head. "I'll be okay. I knew my mama wasn't long for this world. We just thought we had a couple more years together. It was a shock to lose her so abruptly like this. I have no idea what I'll tell Daddy, but I'll figure out something." She blows her nose and puts her car into drive without saying another word.

I can't say I'm sorry to see her drive away down the dirt road, the SUV kicking up shells as it pulls away. The circumstances around Genieve's death don't make much sense. I can't imagine how hard it will be for Jane to grieve and heal from this hellish nightmare. She was already a bitter person. I pray she can find peace and a new lease on life. I know I have.

As horrible as this week has been, I have a feeling that things are on the upturn for my boys and me.

Chapter Twenty-Seven

When we get back to the hotel, Julia Caroline asks for my room key and excuses herself. I'm so tired, but I want to talk to Brian for at least a couple minutes before I go crash. He came here to support me, and that means a lot.

We walk into the lobby and through a sliding glass door to the patio. The glow of the fire pit and streetlights create an enchanting glow. I feel my shoulders relax as we sit down on a cushy outdoor sofa. This is the perfect spot for a cozy chat.

I take Brian's hand in mine and smile. "Thank you for coming here to help us. It's been a weird day to say the very least. How are you feelin' about everything?"

"I'm happy that it seems Carl will leave both of us alone now. Wherever he went, I sure hope he can't come back...same goes for Genieve. She's a real piece of work."

I wipe beads of perspiration from my cheeks. "Whew. You have no idea. We had to leave Beaufort because of the mess she caused when we were young. Little did I know, all the so-called lies were the truth. If I'd only known she and Carl really did have an affair, would I have stayed with him? Was I that afraid to leave him?"

Brian hangs his head down low. "You shouldn't feel bad about wanting to trust your husband. Faithfulness should be a given in marriage. What Carl did is unforgivable, and you definitely deserve to be treated better."

What should I say? Brian's words tug at my heart. I don't want to cry in public. With my heavy eyes and the emotion-packed few days, it would be easy to let the floodgates open and not stop.

Instead, I lean toward him and kiss his lips gently. He kisses me back and wraps his arms around my neck, pulling me closer to him. At this point, I'm almost sitting on his lap. My blood is pumping at record speed. I haven't felt this much electricity with a man in years. I don't want it to end. Thank goodness Julia Caroline is here to keep me honest. Otherwise, I might be tempted to spend the night with Brian.

Whew! Simmer down, Nancy Parsons! We've only started dating. I've got to stop this now, or I'll be in dangerous territory. I pull away from Brian and smile, hoping he can't hear my heart pounding. *What a great feeling!* I didn't know if I would experience romance again.

He runs his hand along my jaw and across my lips, and I'm having a difficult time not falling under his spell again.

I grab his hand again. "This has been wonderful, but I'm exhausted. We should probably get some shuteye so we can leave before lunchtime tomorrow. Let's plan a date for when we're back home."

He kisses my hand. "I look forward to it. Goodnight, beautiful." I watch him walk down the hallway to his room, half tempted to follow him, but I think better of it.

Walking to my room, I think about the passionate kiss and look forward to what may come from our relationship. *It's exhilarating to consider!*

When I open the door to my room, Julia Caroline yawns and stretches until her neck pops and cracks like a gunshot. "I always forget I'm getting old. My body reminds me all the time, especially after a day of traipsing around the backcountry like today. I miss our old adventures from when we were younger, but I don't rightly know if I'm cut out for it anymore."

I laugh. "You—give up a chance for adventure? Never!"

She smirks. "True. I may just have to modify the extent of said adventures or invest in ibuprofen and Icy Hot. Speaking of hot adventures, how was your little rendezvous with Brian?" She bats her eyelashes and puffs out her chest.

I cover my mouth in feigned shock. "A lady never speaks about such things."

"I know. That's why I asked you. I don't see a lady in this room." Only my best friend could get away with such a dig—I know she's kidding.

"Hush your filthy mouth!" I grab a pillow off the bed and throw it at her. "Birds of a feather flock together. What does that say about you?"

Julia Caroline's jaw drops, and we laugh so hard I fall off the bed, which only makes us giggle harder. This is a common occurrence for us, especially when we're exhausted. I hope no one reports us to the front desk for being too loud.

When we calm down, Julia Caroline leans toward me. "Really...I want to know. Are you happy? I know a lot of horrible things have happened to you and your family. Are you going to be okay? It's all I want for you."

"I think so," I whisper, rubbing my eyes and thinking about her question. I'll never get over losing Wesley and MaryAnne, but I need to be strong for their children. Now that Carl and Genieve are out of the picture, I know they can't interfere in the boys' lives. That takes huge a load off my shoulders. And there's Brian. Who knows what will come out of our budding romance? I'm excited to see what transpires.

I lie down and cozy up with a stack of goose down pillows and the freshly laundered duvet on my bed. As I reach to turn off the bedside table lap, Julia Caroline lets out a yawn that echoes through our tiny room, bringing me back from my thoughts.

I shush her. "Ma'am, you are louder than a herd of nanny goats in heat. You're going to wake up the darn whole hotel."

We laugh again but with less intensity. When I catch my breath, I look over at my best friend. "Thank you for saving my butt yet again. You're always there when I need you. I hope I can return the favor someday. Love ya."

Julia Caroline grins ear to ear. "You make life interesting and worth living. I wouldn't want to go down this road without you. Love you, too, sister."

Chapter Twenty-Eight

When we wake up, I run around the room collecting and packing up my other belongings that Jane must have missed when she ransacked the place. Nothing she took to Genieve's house is irreplaceable or worth the headache of dealing with Jane again.

We need to hit the road. I'm so ready to see my babies. From what Julia Caroline said, poor little Clint sounds especially worried. If we stop somewhere, I should pick up presents for them.

Thinking of gifts makes me remember losing my mama's charm, and my stomach hurts. Maybe we should retrace our steps and try looking for it in the daylight. It's a long shot but still a worthwhile endeavor.

Julia Caroline and I take our bags outside. After I load my bag into my car, I go check on Brian.

When I knock on his door, he answers, looking as stunning as usual in his crisp white polo shirt and khaki pants. Like a true Southern gentleman, he holds the door open for me and invites me inside while he finishes gathering his luggage.

Why are my palms sweating and tingling? It hits me...I haven't been in a man's hotel room in ages. But there's no time for romantic advances with Julia Caroline idling the Thunderbird in the parking lot. I'd better simmer down.

He flashes a dimpled smile, melting my heart. "You look so beautiful today, as always. I know you're going to want to see your grandkids and rest, but would it be alright if I brought y'all dinner this weekend? I fry up fresh fish and shrimp every Saturday. With my family all living out of town, I miss sharing the tradition with them. I'd like to share it with your grandsons and you, if that's alright."

I grin. "Of course. We'd love to have you over."

What a sweet and considerate man to include the boys. Will I ever get used to his genteel ways? I'll always try not to take them for granted. I know firsthand what having an unsupportive partner is like. I never want to go back.

After Brian finishes packing, we turn in our hotel room keys at the lobby and join Julia Caroline outside.

"I guess I'll see you two lovebirds back on the island." She winks. I blush and hope Brian doesn't notice. "Hey, is there anywhere y'all want to stop before we go home?"

Brian shakes his head, and I explain my hopefulness for finding the charm in the daylight. "Maybe I'm crazy, but I don't want to go home without at least trying."

Julia Caroline and Brian both nod, and we set course for the Waters' family burial ground.

The twisted oak tree branches cast eerie shadows on the road, and the Spanish moss swirls like fingers reaching for something they've lost. *I know the feeling.* A familiar icy chill reverberates through my body, and I try to keep my teeth from chattering as I drive.

When I pull up to the shack, I park quickly and run toward the water, stopping at the headstones. The large stone slab remains with no sign of the enclosure where we placed the small stone marker or the charm. I run my hands along the smooth surface, hoping to find a hidden groove or lever. After a few minutes, I give up and get on my hands and knees, searching the base of the stone for any sign of my heirloom.

Digging through piles of gritty sand mixed with pine needles and leaves, I smack the ground and growl. There's no sign of anything out of the ordinary. It's as if the stone has stood there just like that for centuries. It's strange to think Carl and Genieve carried the charm to the Other Side for eternity, but they must have.

My throat tightens. What if Mama was the one communicating with me through the charm?

The answer lies on the Other Side. Either way, I'll never talk to my mama on this side of Heaven. *I've lost her all over again.* I wipe a tear from my cheek—life is beyond fragile. People and possessions can slip in and out of our lives in the blink of an eye.

The sound of a car door closing catches my attention, and I see Brian walking toward me. I try to gather my bearings and pull myself up off the ground. As my knees creak like a door in a horror movie, I remember how old I am. Why did I think I could crawl around on the ground like a youngster? Shoot...I hope Brian can't hear the horrific sound effects as I stand.

"Any luck?"

I shake my head and shrug because I'm out of breath. Please, Lord, don't let him ask me another question right now. Panting like a porch dog in the dead heat of July isn't a good look for anyone. And if I try to hold in my labored breathing much longer, I'm going to pass out!

Luckily, he turns his back to me to look around the headstones and the exposed tree roots for a few minutes, giving me a chance to recover. I watch him dig through all the pine needles and leaves I stirred up earlier and stop to examine something.

Did he find the charm? No way! I just dug through that mess!

I run over to join him and get a closer look at what has captured his attention. Brian is cradling a small but intact oyster shell in his hands. *What is so special about it? Don't get me wrong, we love our oysters in the Lowcountry, but their shells are a dime a dozen on any sandy beach or pluff mud bank.*

He flips the shell over to reveal water and tree carvings. "Why do you reckon someone marked up this shell like that?"

"It's beyond me, but I think we should open it to see if there's something inside." I hold out my hand, and he places the shell in my palm. There's a sliver of an opening, and I try pulling the sides apart. It doesn't want to give.

Where is my trusty oyster knife when I need it? I look for a makeshift tool and find a small flat but sturdy stone. *This should do it.*

I wiggle the stone back and forth inside the shell until I feel the sides loosen. After a few more tries, it pops open, and a pink piece of paper falls out. My hands shake as I pick up the miniature scroll off the ground. *Is this a note from Mama?*

Unraveling the paper, I read the words scrolled across it —

"Don't cry for what is lost. Feel joy for what has been found. Everything comes with a cost. Now you're free to find happiness abound. Go home and build the life you deserve."

I hold the note to my chest and send a silent thank you up to Heaven. Whoever my messenger is, God saw fit to let them communicate with me. And they couldn't be more right. I'm surrounded by loving friends and my wonderful grandchildren. What a blessing to have all of them!

Brian asks to see the note. When I place it in his hands, he smiles. "I hope I'm part of 'what has been found' and the 'happiness abound.' If I haven't made it clear, I want to be part of your life."

If my feet are still touching the ground, I'm unaware. *This man makes my heart happy.* I kiss his cheek and grab his hand as we walk back toward the car. Before we climb inside, Julia Caroline leans outside the Thunderbird's driver side window and gives me a knowing look.

"Is everything all good?"

I smile. "Absolutely! Now, it's time to go see my boys and give each of them a giant bear hug." I start to tell Julia Caroline we're going stop, so I can buy them presents. But the perfect gift occurs to me, and it won't cost me a penny, at least not until I'm back on the island.

Sketching on a napkin from my purse, I devise a scavenger hunt for all the kids, including Julia Caroline's granddaughters. They're going to love this. I can't wait to see the young'uns running around looking for the next clue. It will be more exhilarating than the scavenger hunt my messenger took me on, no doubt about that.

After I finish my plan, I smile. *Yes! We're gonna have so much fun together. Lord knows we need it after everything we've been through lately.*

Chapter Twenty-Nine

As I drive, I glance over at Brian, wishing I could lean on his shoulder. The low hum of the car engine hypnotizes me while the warm cross breeze from the open windows soothes my nerves.

I breathe in and appreciate the moment of pure bliss. *Why did I deny myself happiness with a romantic partner for so many years? Fear of rejection, abuse, or neglect? Probably.*

Once you've lived through years of abuse and terror, the trauma doesn't just fade away. I spent years building up confidence in myself and my value. I knew I was a catch, but I didn't think anyone would love, adore, support, or respect me the way I deserved.

Brian is the whole package—he's caring, intelligent, and supportive. *It doesn't hurt that he looks pretty darn good for someone in their fifties. Best of all, he's nothing like Carl.* We're just starting our relationship, but I still can't believe my luck at a second chance with Brian. For some reason, he adores me. I can't wait to kiss him again. My mouth quivers at the thought, but I push it aside. For now, I grab his hand and weave my fingers into his. He smiles, and it's contagious.

The rest of the short trip home is a blur of sweet exchanges with Brian. When we cross the Isle of Palms Connector from Mount Pleasant, my heart overflows with joy. I've missed my little guys somethin' fierce. Even though they've been in good hands with Susan and Jeremy, I couldn't help but worry about them. They've been through so much.

When we pull into the drive, I get a burst of energy and can hardly to park. The second the vehicle stops, I open my door and run inside the house.

Clint is sitting on the couch, holding Blake's hand. *Oh, my goodness—this is the sweetest moment ever.* I don't want to disrupt them, so keep walking toward the kitchen, where I can hear Susan and Jeremy talking, but Clint shrieks, "Nana!"

I turn around to see my sensitive guy with tears in his eyes, and I hug him. My heart sinks. I shouldn't have left my babies, but I had to protect them and myself, so I can be the best Nana possible. Being a caregiver is full of many complex decisions and conflicting priorities. All I can do is try to make the right choices and pray things will work out for our family.

He pulls away and frowns. "Why didn't you call me? I was so worried something bad happened to you like my mom and dad." His chin trembles. Well, that ripped the heck out of my heart.

"I'm so sorry, baby. I was out in the middle of nowhere without a phone. I wanted to call. I really missed you and your brothers, and I hated being away." I pull him close again and kiss his cheek. "Are you doing okay? Have you had a good time with Blake?"

"Yeah. We've been swimming and looking for turtle nests to check on the babies just like Mama taught us. But, Nana—"

"Yes, honey?"

"Someone's been watching me."

My throat tightens. Could Carl have come back? Did he plan to harm the children? What kind of sadistic son of a biscuit eater could dream of hurting his grandbabies?

I draw a deep breath and try to hide my anxiety. "What does this person look like? Have they said anything?"

"I haven't seen or heard them. I can just feel them. It feels heavy like there's a brick on my shoulders."

That doesn't completely calm my nerves, but at least there's a chance it isn't Carl seeking revenge for what happened in Beaufort. I wish Clint didn't have the gift to experience such things, but I remind myself it may be a temporary curse. Children are more open to the paranormal world than most adults. By the time they're ten years old, their openness tends to dwindle, and they become as closed minded as the rest of us.

"If you see or hear anything...anything at all, come get me. It doesn't matter what time—even in the middle of the night. Okay?"

Clint nods, runs back to the couch, and plops down beside Blake. She grabs his hand again. The way these two smile at each other—everyone should experience such an incredible friendship in their lives.

Now that I know Clint is okay, I go into the kitchen to talk to Susan and Jeremy, who are cooking enough food for an army. Between both families, we have eight hungry children ready for breakfast.

After I kiss each of my babies and hug the Nelson girls, I help Susan serve heaping plates of French toast and sausage links to the older kids.

Jeremy hands me a bottle of formula for the baby. "I figured Nana might want to do the honors. I'm sure you've been missing this lil' guy."

"I sure have." I pick up the baby from his highchair and cradle him. His big blue eyes sparkle when he sees me, and I hold back tears as I position the bottle to feed him. Goodness, these boys sure know how to make me feel loved. I suppose they learned from the best—their parents raised them up right.

After everyone finishes breakfast, I gather the children in the living room.

"I have something fun planned for all of us. We're going to divide into three teams and look for items. Each clue will take us to a new place, where I'll share the next clue. Whichever group finds everything wins. The winning team gets to choose our dinner and dessert tonight. Anything goes. Everyone ready?" I divvy up everyone into groups, so there's an adult and at least one older child to help lead the way throughout the scavenger hunt.

Clint stomps forward and grins. "If I win, I want chocolate ice cream for dinner and strawberry cake for dessert."

I laugh. "Okay, buddy. Let's get started. The first thing we need to find is something with stripes on it. This one's easy because you can look for it in the house. Remember to stay with your group the whole time no matter what. Adults, please bring your groups back in fifteen minutes. The baby and I will wait here for you. On your mark, get set, go!"

The groups' footsteps thunder to each far corner of the house, followed by laughing and a series of crashes.

I cringe. *The house is going to look like a tornado hit it after the scavenger hunt. But the memories we're making are more than worth the aftermath.*

I snuggle the baby again. He coos and blows the most adorable raspberries. *Aww—my heart!* I whisper a silent prayer, "Thank you, Lord, for bringing me home to my sweet boys and keeping us all safe and sound. I cannot imagine life without them, and I'm grateful for the opportunity to love and raise them. What a blessing you've given me. In Jesus' name. Amen."

Moments later, the groups gather in the living room again. Clint lunges toward me, wearing a red and navy striped tie I can only assume belonged to Wesley around his forehead. "I'm the Karate Kid—Heee-yaaah!" He kicks and punches the air, and everyone claps.

Blake models one of my striped scarves, which she has fashioned into a sarong. Her younger sister, Elaina, is wearing bright red sunglasses, with a navy and white striped towel slung over her shoulder and zinc oxide on her nose. These kids are so creative!

"Wow! Y'all look fantastic. I didn't expect a fashion show, just for you to find something to share with us. Great work!"

The kids beam and continue strutting around in their

colorful costumes. I cough to cover a giggle. They're way too cute for their own good, and they know it. Little stinkers!

I whistle to get everyone's attention. "Okay, we're ready to move on now. The next item you're looking for is in the backyard. Go find a leaf, rock or stick that looks like something else — an animal or a shape — use your imagination and have fun!"

Everyone scatters again. Blake jumps up and down every time she finds something interesting, and Clint high fives Jeremy every so often. When Julia Caroline's group finishes the challenge, she joins me on the sidelines.

"Nan—this was a great idea. The kids are having so much fun. Is there really going to be just one winning team?"

"Heavens, no. I wouldn't be able to pick one kid over the other." I laugh. "I'll let each of them choose one part of dinner tonight. They all love each other so much. I don't think there's any real competition among them, at least not yet. When they get older, that might change."

Julia Caroline places her hand over her chest. "I hope not. I love this innocent age, especially seeing Clint and Blake holding hands. It's the sweetest thing ever."

"I agree. They're just babies now, but it would be incredible if they stay friends and see what else happens when they get much, much older. We're all family, but wouldn't it be somethin' if these two made it official?"

"It certainly would," Julia Caroline said. "We'll just have to wait and see what transpires after they graduate from high school. Will they go to college, trade school, have careers, travel, or whatever? They have a long time to figure it out."

Oh, to be young!

Chapter Thirty

After spending half an hour or so exploring the vast backyard, the children bring me a double-heart-shaped leaf, a small tree branch twisted into the letter "T," and a white stone shaped like a T-Rex's head.

I cheer and let out a wolf whistle. "You guys knocked it out of the park again! I love the imagination you used to find these things! Let's take a quick break, and we'll regroup for one more challenge in about ten minutes."

The children run laps around the yard, laughing and yelling at each other. It must be nice to have a never-ending supply of energy! Meanwhile, I'm fanning myself with a large empty seed packet from the garden without much success.

Julia Caroline and I go inside to get popsicles and Kool-Aid for the kids and a pitcher of sweet tea along with some peach scones for the adults. Whether the kids realize it, we all need some cold refreshments after running around outside.

Now that everyone is hydrated, I motion for them to step closer. "We're going to the beach for the last part of the scavenger hunt. It's very important that everyone sticks together. Hold hands with the adult in your group and don't wander off alone. I want everyone to have a fair shot. I'll wait until we're all over there to tell you what we're looking for this time."

I pick up the baby and follow everyone else to the powdery, grayish-white sand. The ocean breeze softens the sun's rays as we approach the beach.

When everyone gathers around me, I smile. "This is our last scavenger hunt item to find. I want you to look for something–a seashell, a rock, a piece of driftwood or a chunk of sea glass. Come back in an hour with your favorite piece. We'll do a craft project with whatever you find tomorrow, and you can give it to whomever you'd like."

The ocean's waves peacefully lap onto the sand instead of their typical violent crashing against the shoreline. Maybe there's some hope the children will find intact shells today.

Each group wanders the beach and wades ankle deep in the ocean. Susan, Jeremy and Julia Caroline are laser-focused on the children's every move to make sure no one is swept away. I'm watching, too, from a few feet back. With the baby sleeping on my shoulder, I don't want to trip over a rock or a rogue wave.

The kids pick up shells, palm fronds and other pieces of nature's bounty. Laughter and seagull cries fill the salty air. With the ocean's gently rolling waves and the blue sky, it's the perfect beach day.

My heart swells with gratitude again; I'll hold on to this beautiful memory forever. *Geez...I'm really turning into a sentimental old woman, but I'm okay with that.*

I take a quick count of our kiddos. Three of the boys are splashing Susan, and the girls are examining their finds with Jeremy. *Wait—where's Clint? I can't find him in the group. I'm sure he's out there with the other kids. I probably can't see him from this angle. That must be it, but I'm not taking a chance.* I run closer. *Still no sign of my little buddy.*

Julia Caroline joins me. "What's the matter?"

"Where's Clint? He's not with everyone else down here."

"He said you asked him to go home. I watched him walk back inside. Didn't you talk to him?"

My blood turns cold. "No. I didn't, and it's not like Clint to lie. There must be something else going on. He mentioned someone was watching him. Do you think Carl has come back and is messing with us?"

Julia Caroline takes the baby out of my arms. "Go to the house now! I'll be right behind you as soon as I hand the baby to Susan. Be prepared to recite Bible verses and take my cross pendant. That should work as a temporary fix at least." She slips the chain from around her neck and hands me the pendant. "Be careful!"

I turn to run toward the house. *How dare Carl come back again. If it's the last thing I do, I'll make him regret bringing innocent, sweet Clint into this horrible situation.*

Grr! I punch the air as I climb the steps up to the boardwalk that leads to the house. Huffing and puffing, *I'm ready to take on this monster. I have no fear this time.*

God is on my side, and that's all I need to know.

When I reach the door, I look inside. Clint is sitting on the living room sofa, but I can't tell if anyone is with him. My pulse normalizes a little bit, knowing he is okay. But I'm afraid what Carl has said or done to my boy. I take a deep breath and enter the house.

I tiptoe closer, hoping for a chance to assess the situation before Carl sees me. When I hide behind a corner in the foyer, I don't see anyone sitting with Clint.

Well, this is a head scratcher!

I walk into the living room and sit down beside him. "Young man, why did you tell Ms. Julia Caroline I told you to come back to the house?"

Clint shrugs. "Because you did, Nana. I followed you back here, and you gave me this."

He opens his tiny hand, and there sits my mama's charm in all its tarnished silver glory. Heat rises up my chest and neck, and the room begins spinning. *I don't know which way is up or down. I certainly didn't tell Clint to go home or hand him the charm.*

My tongue is heavy, but I manage to speak slowly. "Where...

where did you find that? Please tell me the truth." I hold my head, hoping to stop the spinning.

"Ma'am, I already told ya. I promise it's the truth. I ain't never lied to you." Clint's eyes tear up, and I feel horrible because I believe him. What can I say to this child when I don't understand what is happening?

Julia Caroline rushes into the living room. "Did he leave already? Good job, Nan!"

I lie down on the floor pushing down stomach bile that threatens to erupt. *Have I followed the White Rabbit down the hole to Wonderland? Maybe I'll spend the rest of my life locked up in an institution.* A cool blast from the air vents helps me fight the impending nausea.

Clint, sobbing, hands Julia Caroline the charm before running to his room and slamming the door behind him.

I cry, too. "I've hurt that boy again. Something fishy is going on, but I didn't get my conversation with Clint right at all. I made him feel like I don't believe a word he says. Someone told him to come back here, and he thought it was me. They gave him the charm. I believe him, but how can that be?"

Chapter Thirty-One

S usan and Jeremy offer to take the kids over to Julia Caroline's house for the night. I thank them and promise to return the favor when they need a babysitter. I hope my brilliant best friend and I can solve the mystery who might be my imposter and why they'd bother with the illusion.

Carl couldn't pull off looking like a woman, no matter how hard he tried. Julia Caroline pointed out that Genieve, with all her plastic surgery and blonde hair dye, couldn't look more different from me. Hopefully, that means those other two have gone on to the Other Side for good. *We don't need any more frustration from them.*

Could it be one of my friends with a similar look? I mean all middle-aged women with short graying hair look the same when they're wearing a white button-down swim coverup, sunglasses and an oversized straw sun visor. I don't think any of them would send him home with me sitting on the beach just a few feet away. Plus, we would have seen and heard any of those women talking to him from a mile away. None of my friends are exactly what you'd call quiet.

Then, who is this mystery woman who is messing with my

grandson and bringing back heirlooms from the great beyond? I'm grateful to have my mama's charm back, but I wish the circumstances were less bizarre.

After nodding off twice as we talk, Julia Caroline heads to the spare twin bed in my room and collapses on the mattress. I follow her to my room, but my mind won't slow down despite it being 2:30 in the morning. My stomach aches every time I think of hurting Clint's feelings.

Julia Caroline flips on the nightstand lamp near her bed and sighs. "I can hear you thrashing around over there. What's on your mind?" I lie still and stay silent, hoping she'll give up and turn off the light again. "Nan, I know you're awake—so spill it."

I kick the mattress. "Dang it. Can't I lie here in my misery? I'm not going to be up for Grandmother of the Year, am I? I've failed these children a million ways to Sunday. Clint won't ever forgive me for not believing him. What am I going to do? Be honest—am I too old or ill-equipped to raise all these children all by myself?"

She shoots straight up in bed and shakes her finger at me. "Nancy Parsons! You take that back right now. You are being a mom, dad, and a mighty fine Nana to boot, to these kids. They couldn't be more loved. You're just exhausted from going from one end of Beaufort to the other, and back home. So, you're not thinking clearly. Please take a deep breath and remember how much you love each other. And don't forget—Wesley and Mary-Anne chose you out of everyone they knew to be their children's guardian. Is it going to be easy raising five boys as a single woman? No, but you have me. I'll always be here for you."

I try to listen objectively and take the words to heart. But my mind is laser focused on Clint. I know I'll feel better when I can apologize to him for the whole darn misunderstanding. Regardless of who the imposter is, my grandbaby thought he was obeying my request. I need him to understand I don't blame him —he did nothing wrong.

Julia Caroline scrunches up her face. "Look, we've all made mistakes as parents and grandparents at some point. Think back to raising Wesley. I'm sure you made some parenting decisions you regretted, but no one can dispute he turned out to be a fine man and a police chief of all things."

"Dang it all! Why are you always right? It's so … so … infuriating!" I ball my fists and let out a low growl.

"Calm down, there. It's hard right now because you're getting into the flow of things. I'm always here for you. I know your family members and mine are happy to help anytime. Why don't you go back to work part time when school starts again. You need some space to be Nancy Parsons, not just Nana to five little boys. And part of being you should also include dating Brian. You two are good together."

I roll my eyes. "Now you're just adding insult to injury." I clutch my chest, close my eyes and pretend to die.

Julia Caroline shakes her head and laughs. "You're too much, but I'm glad to hear you joking around again. Life has been strange lately, but we'll figure it out together. Now, let's go to sleep for real this time." She leans over and turns off the light.

I settle into the bed, and the pillow caresses my head. Tension melts from my shoulders, and I let the rest of my body relax.

Maybe it will be okay, but we need to find out who is impersonating me. It could be dangerous for Clint and the other children to take directions from a stranger.

As I drift off to sleep, I dream of Clint on the beach, holding the charm in his hand. He looks up at a woman and smiles. I can't see her face, but I recognize the wedding band on her ring finger. The woman pats his head and points toward the house. Clint smiles and nods before running toward the boardwalk. About halfway down the wooden planks, he looks back where the woman stood, but she is gone.

This time, it's my turn to cut on the lamp. Julia Caroline mumbles and motions for me to turn off the light.

"No, ma'am. I need to talk. Wake up right now!"

She rubs her eyes and stares at me. "Good gravy, what could be so important? We've barely slept for days, woman! I could hear you snoring like a trombone over there, so I know you fell asleep."

"You're not going to believe it. I had a dream about Clint and the mystery woman. I think I know who she is. Maybe my unconscious told me through the dream, or maybe she planted it there herself. I don't understand how these spooky things work. Do you know if that's even possible?"

Julia Caroline yawns. "You're not making a bit of sense right now. Let's try this again in the morning."

"But..." I throw my hands in the air.

Julia Caroline pulls an invisible zipper across her mouth. "Zip it, Nan. I can't do this right now. I feel like a semi-truck ran over me, put it in reverse and repeated the process about twenty times. Now, it's time for my beauty sleep before I turn into a pumpkin."

She shuts off the light, and I hear her breathing even out almost instantly. How is she asleep again already?

Defeated, I flop back on the mattress. Well, there's no going back to sleep now. I get up out of bed and pad downstairs to the kitchen table. Picking up the charm, I say a prayer for a miracle. I open the charm, and a sliver of pink paper waits inside. Thank you, Lord!

My hands shake as I remove it from the metal chamber. *Will this note confirm my dream and suspicions?*

Chapter Thirty-Two

I hold the piece of paper close to my heart and close my eyes. *What a sweet moment — one I want to remember for the rest of my life.*

Unraveling the scroll, my voice shakes as I read the words:

"Your mama traveled from this side of Heaven to return the charm you loved so. She is not your messenger. When the time is right, I'll reveal myself."

For an hour, I sit at the kitchen table and stare at the words. This person confirmed the accuracy of my dream. The reason Clint thought I was the one who gave him the charm is it was my mama. People have always commented on our resemblance.

When she died, she was in her mid-fifties. I shiver, considering she was only a few years older than me. It was devastating losing her so young.

I wish she could have stayed here long enough to say hello to me, but if I'm honest, it would have hurt to watch her vanish into thin air. She made the right decision to leave the charm with my sweet little guy.

Fighting my emotions, I make a cup of chamomile tea and take it to the living room sofa, where I lie down to read a book by my favorite author, Dorothea Benton Frank. Dottie lives across Breach Inlet in a beautiful home on Sullivan's Island. She describes our beautiful sister islands like no one else. And I love the characters she creates.

After a few chapters, even DBF's fab writing can't entice my heavy eyes to stay open. I finally drift off and sleep without stirring for hours.

The herd of wild elephants, err ... I mean rambunctious children, stomping through the front door wakes me. Clint comes inside last, hanging his head as he enters. I can't stand it another minute. *We have to talk now.*

Julia Caroline, Susan and Jeremy take the other kids to the backyard, and I ask Clint to go with me to the front porch. He trudges the whole way outside. Watching him frown as he plops down at the top of the steps breaks my heart. I hope I can regain his trust.

I sit down next to him and hold his hand. "Sweetie, I want to apologize for our misunderstanding yesterday. I love you and your brothers more than anything in the world. You can tell me anything, and I promise to be a better listener. I was tired, but that's no excuse. I will do better. I promise."

I squeeze him tight and kiss his forehead.

He pulls back. "But Nana, why do you not remember telling me to come home yesterday? Do you have alls-timers like my grandpa did?"

Tears fill his eyes, breaking my heart. MaryAnne's father was diagnosed with early onset Alzheimer's a few years ago and died from a stroke last year. Poor Clint has experienced so much loss in a short period. I wish I could wave a magic wand and bring back all these incredible people so they could spend time with our boys.

Clint shakes my arm. "Nana?"

"Sorry, baby. No. I don't have Alzheimer's. But I have an explanation for what happened. I need to tell you something that might be hard to believe. Do you trust me?"

He wipes his nose on his sleeve and nods furiously. "Yeppers."

I hold my breath...ugh...here goes. "The person who told you to come home was my mama, your great grandmother."

Clint winces and scratches his head. "But I thought she died way before I was born. How could she come here?"

I gulp. "I can't explain how she came here from Heaven. All I know is she did."

He sits there, and I can see the wheels turning in his head. What else can I tell him to help this make sense? I feel unprepared for this scenario. As far as I know, Wesley never encountered spirits. But Wesley didn't experience a great loss to spur an ability to see and communicate with the dead.

I rub Clint's hand. "Do you understand? Do you have any questions? I'll try to answer if I can."

"Nana, Great Gramma was so nice. She gave me a big hug and told me I look just like my daddy."

"Honey, I'm so glad you got to see her! And she's right—you're the spitting image of Wesley, well, most of the time. I can see your beautiful mama in your eyes. You're blessed with both of their good looks."

He puts his hands in his pockets and flashes a dimpled grin. "Did you get to see her, too?"

I look away and try to hide my disappointment. "No—I didn't, sweetie. I wish I could have."

He nods. "I miss my mama, too. But I'm glad they're in Heaven together. That makes me feel better knowing Great Gramma is there to take care of Daddy and Mama. I know God is taking care of them, but he's gotta be pretty busy all the time."

A mix of emotions overwhelm me, and my nervous energy boils over. I laugh so I don't cry. Clint starts fidgeting. This has been an extraordinarily long, heavy conversation for a child.

"Honey, you can go play with the other kids. No need to stay here with this old woman when there are water balloons to pop in the backyard."

Clint's eyes widen and he runs outside to join the rest of the gang. I watch them play from the open kitchen window. Their giggles fill the air as they chase each other around the yard. I'm grateful for this moment of peace and fun for my little guys.

Julia Caroline comes inside to get some lemonade and cookies for everyone to enjoy outside.

After she pulls everything together, she stares at me. "Clint seems okay now, but you don't. What's the matter? Don't tell me there isn't something else wrong."

I don't say anything, and she throws her hands in the air. "You know I'll just keep pushing until you tell me."

Tears sting my eyes. "Is it wrong I'm upset Mama didn't come see me before she went back to the Other Side? I would have given anything for just a minute with her. I feel selfish thinking it, though." I wipe a tear from my cheek.

"Of course not. I would think something was wrong if you didn't feel that way. I'd give anything to see my mama again. And you've had a horrendous year. A moment with your mother would have given you a little bit of comfort when all hell has broken loose. You deserve that. But don't lose hope. We have no idea how her comings and goings might work. Who's to say she won't come back?"

Julia Caroline picks up a tray of cookies and a pitcher of lemonade and heads outside to feed everyone. With one foot propping the screen door open, she turns back to offer more advice. "You have her charm again. Send a note to your messenger. It doesn't have to be a one-way conversation, ya know? Then, come outside and play with these adorable kids."

Unsurprisingly, she has a point—I should try sending a note. I walk over to MaryAnne's writing desk to find a pen and a pink memo pad, tearing off the corner of one page. How can I fit every-thing I want to say on such a tiny scrap?

I stare at the paper for a minute, mentally drafting my message before covering both sides with my note:

"Thank you for helping protect these boys. I want nothing but the best for them. They've been through an awful lot, and I think it was reassuring to Clint he got to meet my mama. Could you let her know I would love even a brief moment with her?"

The words punch me in the gut as I roll the paper into a tight scroll and place it inside the charm. I could throw up. What do I do now? This is my first message to Heaven, other than my prayers, which I know beyond a shadow of a doubt go straight to God.

That's it! When in doubt...pray...always! I whisper my prayer, "Lord, please help this note find its way to my messenger, our guardian angel. They have helped me see the forest through the trees and navigate these muddy waters. Thy will be done. In Jesus' name, Amen."

Chapter Thirty-Three

The next two weeks fly by. Susan, Jeremy, and their girls return to their home in Tennessee to get ready for the school year. Our household shifts gears, as well, buying backpacks, notebooks, pencils, and new clothing.

With the triplets starting kindergarten this year, that will only leave the baby at home with me. He'll be old enough for mother's day out in a couple months, so I've started looking into the best options nearby. Julia Caroline offered to keep him while I work, but I want to spend as much time as possible with all the kids as the older ones adjust to their classes and homework.

I can always pick up work as a caterer, cook, or waitress. I learned a long time ago—if you're willing to work hard, you'll never starve on this island, especially during tourist season.

School starts tomorrow, so I sit down with the older boys and help them load notebook paper into folders and sharpen their pencils. I'd forgotten how busy this time of year is for students and parents, but I'm excited for the boys to meet their teachers and classmates.

After Clint fills his backpack with supplies, he frowns. "Nana, do we really have to go back to school? Mama always sang us a song before I went to school on the first day. I don't wanna go back there without her song. I want my mama to walk me into my classroom and tell the teacher my name. I need her to kiss me goodbye." He folds his arms across his chest and pouts.

A lump forms in my throat. I try coughing, but I can't make words come out, so I pull him close to me and smooth his hair. Finally, the words come to me.

"Honey, we'll never be able to bring your mama back. I wish we could more than anything in the world. I would gladly trade places with her, so you could be together. But know I love you and your brothers so much it hurts. If you teach me the song, I can sing it for you. Do you know the words?"

"No! You can't sing to me, only Mama can!"

Clint breaks free from my arms and stomps upstairs to his room, slamming the door behind him. The other boys stare at me. My guts are churning, but I have to hold it together for them.

"Don't worry. He'll be okay." As the words leave my mouth, I hope they are true. I can't let the other kids, or myself, spiral. We need a distraction right now. "Hey! Who wants to make cookies?"

The triplets jump up and down and the baby claps. I'll take that as a yes.

We move into the kitchen and pull all the ingredients out of the cupboard and refrigerator. Once I combine everything in a mixing bowl, I preheat the oven and let each of the triplets take a turn stirring up the dough. Then, I show them how to scoop out cookies onto the baking sheet.

After I place the cookie sheet in the oven, I send the boys to watch cartoons in the living room, promising to bring them cookies as soon as they're ready.

I take a few minutes to do dishes and wipe down the countertops. The tantalizing scent of brown sugar combining with chocolate makes my mouth water. When will those darn things be done? Just four minutes left on the timer.

Staring out the window, I see Clint walking around the backyard. When did he go outside? I don't let the boys wander around outside alone, especially without asking me first. Clint knows better than to talk to a stranger. I hear his voice, but I don't see anyone. Who is out there with him? My pulse races. If someone is messing with him, they're going to regret it.

I grab a knife from a kitchen drawer. Holding my breath, I walk outside and peer around the corner. Clint is swinging on the swing set, his feet not touching the ground once as he's propelled higher and higher. What is happening here?

Clint's boisterous giggles reassure me he feels safe, but should he? Who or what is pushing the dang swing?

Regardless, the knife won't do me much good in defending us in this case. I place it on the window ledge and approach the swing set. My nerves are shot, but I need to take a measured approach.

I draw a deep breath. "Clint, honey, were you talking to someone?"

The swing comes to a dead stop. Clint groans and looks behind him. "Hey! Why did you stop pushing me?"

I gulp. He sees someone I can't. This never occurred to me as a possibility. After seeing Carl, I thought I'd be able to see and communicate with all spirits. How can I protect Clint if I can't see everyone he's interacting with?

Clint screams and points toward the house. "Nana! Look —fire!"

I turn around to see smoke seeping through the kitchen window. Oh, no! I forgot about the cookies! The other children are in the living room. If I go around to the front door, I can get the boys outside without walking through the billowing smoke.

I look Clint in the eyes. "Can you go tell Julia Caroline we need the fire department here right now? Be sure to look both ways before you cross the street." He nods and takes off. Under ordinary circumstances, I wouldn't send him alone across busy Palm Boulevard, but I know he can handle it. Besides, I don't have much choice right now.

Running to the front yard, I pray for my boys' safety first and foremost. But I also hope we can save their home, along with family mementos and photos to remind them of their parents.

As I round the corner from the side of the house, a hole in the sand catches my foot, twisting my ankle. A crunching sound ricochets off the cluster of oak trees, and I let out a scream. I try standing, and pain shoots up my entire foot. Dang it all! Only I could break a bone during the middle of another crisis.

Sweat beads across my brow as I crawl on my hands and knees toward the front door. I will get my little guys out of this fire if it's the last thing I do.

My hands cut from the shells and debris in the sand, I finally make it to the steps. I pull myself up and use the handrails on either side to hold my weight. Panting, I pull my body up eight steps. I'm on the wrong side of forty-nine for this sort of athleticism. I sure wish I was about twenty years younger right now.

When I reach the top of the steps, I use the long tail of my shirt to protect my hand when turning the doorknob. Thank goodness, it isn't sizzling hot yet. I draw a deep breath and brace myself for the scene awaiting me in the living room.

By some miracle, the fire has been contained to the corner of the kitchen where the stove sits. I let out a sigh of relief and thank God at the sight of four sweet little boys lying on the sofa asleep. They haven't noticed a thing is wrong.

I wake the triplets, tell them to run outside quickly and sit together on the sand away from the house. Then, I scoop up the baby and follow them outside. God and my guardian angel are the only way I made it out of there with an ankle injury and four children in tow. Praise the Lord! I whisper a prayer that Clint is with Julia Caroline, and help is one the way.

I'm sure that's the case, but I have no way of knowing how long it will take them to arrive. I need to go back inside to save the house and my family's belongings, regardless of my injury. Being a first responder, Wesley always kept plenty of fire extinguishers around their house. I can easily get to the ones in the living room without needing to go into the depths of the kitchen.

With my heart racing, I help the triplets settle into a safe far spot away from the house and hand them the baby.

"Do not leave here until Julia Caroline, a firefighter, or I tell you it's okay. And keep your little brother safe. Understand me?"

They nod, and the gravity of the situation must have hit them because all three of the older boys' lips begin trembling.

"Everything's going to be okay. I just have to go put out the fire in the kitchen, so it doesn't spread. I'll be back as soon as I can."

Now that I know all of the kids are out of the house, a sense of calmness...maybe it's adrenaline...overcomes me. Getting up the stairs and into the house goes much easier this time. I grab two fire extinguishers from entryway coat closet, prop myself up against a chair, and start spraying the foam toward the burning oven. It doesn't make much difference, so I move my focus to the edges of the smaller flames lining the countertops closest to the living room.

If I can just contain the fire to the kitchen until the firefighters get here, we can always rebuild one room. Wesley and Mary-Anne's mementos and the children's belongings are scattered throughout the rest of the house.

Billowing smoke grows thicker by the minute, making it increasingly harder to breathe. In my haste, I didn't think to grab a makeshift mask to cover my nose and mouth. Great job, Nancy. That's fire safety 101, and I just failed. To make matters worse, the second fire extinguisher is empty. Wesley over prepared for every emergency imaginable, but I'm sure he never thought there would be a fire of this magnitude in his home. Why would he?

Shaking off the dizziness that is settling in, I hobble over to the kitchen island and grab the water sprayer from the sink. The stream just barely reaches the flames but seems to help more than the extinguisher.

The combination of sirens wailing in the distance the over-powering scent of burning wood, and the thick blanket of smoke burning my eyes sends me into sensory overload. How much longer can I do this?

Everything goes black, and I feel my body collapse underneath me.

Chapter Thirty-Four

Bright light burns my eyes. I can't focus on the faces in front of me. Something is covering my mouth and nose. I try talking, but no words come. Am I dead? What will happen to the boys now?

"Hey, hey...calm down. It's alright, Nan. You're in the hospital for smoke inhalation, but you're going to be okay. The boys are safe. Just rest."

"Julia Caroline?" My voice is muffled. "Where am I? Why can't I see? I distinctly remember putting in my contacts this morning."

"The paramedics had to take your contacts out to check your eyes for any injuries. Hang on, I have your glasses." She places the black wire frames on my face and straightens them. "There you go, that has to be better. Try not to talk so much with that oxygen mask on. You need to keep breathing in, nice and slow and steady to help your lungs recover. You took in a lot of smoke."

I ignore her command. "Where are the boys? Are they upset?"

"Brian and his daughter are taking care of them at your house. Your niece said she'll check on them later tonight. Don't worry about a thing. They're fine, just worried about you like the rest of us. The doctors and nurses are doing a great job taking care of you so far, though."

Thank goodness the boys are okay. My stomach dips at the thought of the kids worrying about me, but there's not much I can do about that until I talk to them. At least they're in capable hands with Brian and his daughter. The thought of them spending time together warms my heart.

"What about the house?"

Julia Caroline bites her lip. "The entire kitchen wall where the stove was is gone, but the rest can be salvaged. The smoke will take a while to air out, and you're looking at replacing some flooring, paint and other cosmetic repairs." She pauses and looks away. "You kept it from spreading, but you know what? That was the dumbest thing you've done in your entire life. I'm not sure I'll ever forgive you for it. Those kids would have lost the person they love most in the world after having just lost both of their parents. Selfishly, I would have lost my best friend, my sister."

"I'm so sorry," I whisper. "I couldn't face having those children lose the house and everything that reminds them of their parents."

"Understandable, but they need you more than a house, their toys, family pictures or the trinkets Wesley and MaryAnne collected."

I turn my head away and pretend to fall asleep, hoping Julia Caroline will leave. Judgment and a lecture from my best friend is the last thing I want now, no matter how right she is.

While playing opossum, I fall into a deep sleep with vivid dreams of Wesley and MaryAnne dancing at their wedding, followed by the day Clint was born in this very hospital. Both rank high on my list of favorite memories.

Seeing my son and his lovely wife happy will always be a bright point in my life. I can't wait to see my grandchildren find the same happiness.

Perhaps Brian and I will find ours together, as well. He's already made me feel valued and respected. And he's helping with the children now when I need support. My dream turns to our last kiss, and warmth envelopes my body like a cozy quilt on a winter day. Our budding relationship has been an unexpected comfort.

I wake to the whirring of machines and half a dozen people wearing scrubs walking in and out of my room. When a young nurse pauses to check my vitals, I ask when I can take off the oxygen mask.

She goes to get the doctor. A middle-aged man with graying dark hair returns with her, and he smiles.

"Ms. Parsons, we did some blood work while you were unconscious, and I'm happy to report everything looks great. We just want to do some X-rays in the morning to make absolutely sure you're out of the woods before we send you home. I'd consider it a huge favor to me if you'd leave that oxygen mask on tonight while you sleep. Any questions?"

"Can I take it off long enough to call my grandchildren? They were with me during the fire. I know they're worried."

He nods. "Make it quick and try not to upset yourself. You need to keep your breathing steady. The nurse will be back to check on you shortly."

They both leave the room, and I tear the mask from my face. Freedom—even if it's short-lived! Leaning over the bed, I grab the phone to call my house.

Clint answers the phone, and my heart nearly stops. I hadn't expected him to be the one to pick up.

"Hi, sweetie. How are you and your brothers?"

"Nana!" He starts sobbing. "I thought you died in the fire. I was so scc...ar...ed. Are you gonna be okay? Will you come home soon?"

"Yes, honey. The doctor thinks I'm fine. He's going to let me come home tomorrow. Are y'all listening to all the adults who are taking care of you?"

"Yes, ma'am. We are being good. Julia Caroline talked to our teachers. We're gonna stay home from school this week. Nana, I miss you and love you so much."

My heart aches for these kids. I wish they weren't having to miss their first week of school.

"Baby, I love y'all so much. We're going to get our lives together, and everything is gonna be okay. Give your brothers a hug for me and let them know I'll be home tomorrow. Goodnight."

As we hang up, I start to put the mask back on, but I'm tempted to run out of the hospital to take care of my sweet little guys instead. The nurse comes back in my room, and I think better of it as she offers me some water and dinner. I need to rest so I can be strong enough to go home tomorrow.

Chapter Thirty-Five

After taking a few X-rays the next morning, the lab technician wheels me back to my room, where Julia Caroline sits, reading a magazine. She jumps to her feet, making a fuss over my frizzy hair and showing me the clothing she brought for me to put on before we went home.

"I pitched the outfit they brought you here in. It reeked of smoke, and not in a good way like the ribs at Melvin's BBQ."

My stomach rumbles. "Dagnabit, woman! Now I want a whole slab of ribs slathered in sauce and all the fixin's. Why did you have to say that?"

She chuckles and pulls a small paper bag from under her chair. "That reminds me, I stopped by Acme Cantina to get your favorite breakfast — a fried chicken biscuit topped with a fried egg, a side of pimento cheese grits, and one of their strawberry and cream hand pies."

"Bless you. That is the best news since the nurse told me I could take off the darn mask this morning. The hospital food tastes like cardboard covered in moldy sawdust."

After I devour the delicacies from Acme, the doctor comes in to share my X-Ray results.

"Everything looks good, Ms. Parsons. But I need you to promise me you'll leave the firefighting to the professionals in the future. I talked to the fire chief to find out how long you were in house before his team pulled you out. The strange thing is he said you were already outside, lying on the porch when they got there."

I stare at Julia Caroline. "Did you pull me out of the house, or did you see who did?"

She shakes her head. "I got there right after the first fire engine started working on the house. One of the new fire fighters mentioned seeing a younger woman in scrubs by your side as they approached you. We don't know who it was. Clint ran ahead of me, though. Maybe he saw her."

A chill tingles down my spine. Who is this mysterious woman who ran into a burning house to save me? How did she know anyone was inside?

Why risk it all for a stranger? She should have just called 911.

Absent-mindedly, I go through the motions of filling out stacks of patient discharge paperwork. I have to get home to make sure the kids are okay. I know they are being well cared for, but I'm their nana. We need each other. Plus, I want to find out what Clint knows.

While Julia Caroline leaves the room to retrieve her car, a nurse helps me change out of the hospital gown and slip on my clean outfit.

I stand slowly to slip on my pants. Thankfully, my ankle seems to be a lot better now, just a little sore. My injury must have been more minor than I thought.

My eye twitches as I sit down in the wheelchair at the foot of my bed. I'm fine and don't want to ride in this darn thing. I start to protest, but if it would help me leave the hospital faster, I'd ride a starving alligator with an extra row of pointy teeth.

We reach the lobby doors just as Julia Caroline pulls up in the Thunderbird. The nurse helps me to my feet and into the car. I thank her as she closes the door and sink into the cushioned seat.

Julia Caroline smiles. "It's so good to be taking you home,

and I mean your actual home on Palm Court. I didn't blame you for wanting to keep the children in their house, so they could adjust more easily. But now that you've had to move back to your house anyway, don't you think it would be good for us to live in walking distance from each other? I could be of more help. I know James would love having boys close by to play catch when he's around."

I nod. "I would like that, but I should talk to the boys before I decide. I want them to have a say in where they live and what we do with their home. Plus, my house is much smaller. We could make it work, but they wouldn't have their own bedrooms or as much space to play."

"That all makes sense. You're a wonderful, selfless grandmother, and your boys are lucky to have you."

"I love them. I truly can't imagine my life without them."

Moments later, we pull into the driveway at my house. The white cottage shimmers like a pearl in the noon sunlight, and the scent of honeysuckle tickles my nose. There's nothing like being home, especially knowing my babes are safe inside.

Julia Caroline parks as close to the front porch as possible. Even though I tell her I'm fine, she helps me get out of the car, walk into the house and sit down on the couch. The boys run full force and surround me. Clint hugs my neck, dangling his arms over my shoulder. I grab his hand. The other boys jump up and down in a flurry of excitement, and I reach out for each of them, so I can cover their chubby cheeks with kisses.

"I'm so glad to see you all. I think you've each grown about a foot since I've seen you." Clint stands on his tiptoes and stretches his arms up in the air. I laugh. "You're my little comedian."

He bows, and I grin. "Sweetie, did you see someone...a young woman in scrubs helping me get out of the house? A firefighter saw someone with me, but she left when they got there."

Clint looks away, so I ask him again. "Please, honey. Tell me so I can properly thank whoever helped. That's the only reason I want to know. You're not in any sort of trouble or anything like that."

He shifts his weight and shakes his head. "I can't tell you. I promised I wouldn't say anything, not yet. She wants to talk to you first."

"Clint Parsons! I'm your grandmother and legal guardian. I'm in charge of keeping all of us safe. If someone was walking around our property, I need to know. Also, the whole reason I walked outside right before the fire was to see who you were talking to. Wait—was it that woman?"

Clint shrugs. "Nana, would you want me to go back on a promise? Daddy always said a man is only as good as his word."

How am I supposed to respond to this? On one hand, Clint is being stubborn — a trait I don't want to encourage — but on the other, he shouldn't break promises he makes. At least he comes by it honest. His dad was as strong-willed as they come. For that matter, they both may have inherited from me...eek! My cheeks burn at the thought.

"I agree with your dad about keeping promises, but he wouldn't want you to keep secrets from me."

"It's only a secret for right now. She wants to talk to you tonight. I told her you were coming home today when she came to see me this morning."

I pound my fist on the table. "Who came here to see you this morning? How did she know you were here? I don't like the idea of a stranger talking to you without me being around. Please tell me who she is right now!"

Julia Caroline tells Clint to go upstairs and play with his brothers. Once he's out of earshot, she reprimands me.

"You know that boy thinks you hung the moon. Susan and Jeremy wouldn't have let a stranger around the kids, so there must be a reasonable explanation. Give him a chance to talk to you on his terms and timeline. I don't understand why he's being so secretive, but he's a good kid. I'm sure he has a good reason for not spilling the beans right away. If he doesn't tell you tonight, then, be more insistent tomorrow."

I close my eyes and place my reddening face in my hands. Being a parent is harder than I remembered, but it's worth every agonizing second. Clint and his brothers deserve love, patience, and kindness. I need to work on the last two, especially being patient.

Julia Caroline hugs me. "I know this parenting gig is tough. I hope I didn't overstep by saying my piece, but sometimes, it's hard to be objective when you're frustrated as a caregiver. I wanted to make sure you thought through everything before you overreacted with Clint. Bless his heart, he has a fragile soul. If you're okay being her alone for an hour or so, I need to run home to do a few things, but I'll be back in time to help you cook supper."

After we say our goodbyes, I can't seem to get settled. It's time to eat crow and apologize to my sensitive lil' man for the second time this week. I groan. Why is this becoming our norm? It hurts to know how badly I'm failing him. We'll have to grow together.

I walk slowly upstairs, holding onto the railing to make sure I don't re-injure my ankle. When I finally get to the landing, I knock on Clint's door.

He tells me to come in, and I sit down next to him on his bed. "Honey, I'm so sorry. I trust you, but you have to tell me if there is a stranger walking around our house or yard. Since you told me she is going to stop by tonight, I'll wait to talk to her then. Do you understand?"

He nods. "Yep, but she isn't a stranger. She'll be here tonight in the garden. That's all I'm supposed to say."

I force a smile. "I love you. Let me know when she's here."

Chapter Thirty-Six

I spend the rest of the day cleaning out junk drawers and closets as a distraction from thinking about our anticipated guest. Stacks of old clothing and books fill every empty surface in the living room and kitchen. I could probably start a full-blown flea market with this mess.

Julia Caroline rolls her eyes at the tidy piles. "Is this busy work actually helping you not worry about your visitor who's coming over tonight?"

I stick out my tongue, getting a laugh out of her. "No. It isn't, but I need something to keep my hands busy while the children play. Waiting for our visitor is grating on my nerves somethin' fierce."

"Wouldn't doing something fun with them help take your mind off things, too?" Her eyes sparkle with a telling gleam.

"Oh, boy. What cockamamy scheme have you cooked up this time? We can't get into anything too wild right now since our guest could show up at any moment. I don't want the boys to get wound up or dirtier than they already are."

"It isn't anything like that. I found these old home movies at my house, and I thought y'all might like to see them." She holds up a basket filled with VHS tapes. The top two are labeled *Clint's First Birthday* and *Summer Vacation 1989.*

I grab the birthday video and pop it into the VCR player. "Hey, boys. Come see Clint's first birthday party. He was so tiny and adorable!"

Everyone plops down on a sofa, except the baby who is toddling around. When he sees one-year-old Clint on the TV, he does a double take. I laugh. The boy probably hasn't seen someone close to his own age in quite some time. I need to fix that, but he'll be in mother's day out or preschool soon enough.

I can't help but think about how kids at this age don't talk back yet or keep secrets from their grandmothers. Thank goodness!

The boys laugh at Clint in the video. He's walking around with a cone-shaped birthday hat that has fallen to one side of his head. And they gush when he falls asleep while eating ice cream and cake. Such sweet moments.

Of course, it stings to see Wesley and MaryAnne so full of life and love. I knew it would, but I don't want to avoid sharing videos, pictures or memories with the kids no matter how much it hurts me. They deserve to get to know their incredible parents.

When MaryAnne bends over to kiss baby Clint on the forehead in the video, Clint jumps up from the couch and yells, "Mama!" before running outside. I start to follow him, and Julia Caroline grabs my hand.

"I'll get these little guys fed and cleaned up, so you can take your time with Clint. Let me know if you need me."

"Thank you. I honestly don't know what I'd do without you," I murmur on my way outside.

I walk to the backyard, but I don't see Clint in his usual spot where he likes to dig in my empty flower beds with his toy dump trucks and bulldozers. It's unlike him to leave the yard without permission, so I move toward the wooded corner of the yard just beyond my potting shed.

"Clint, honey, where are you?"

No answer. My stomach drops—where did this kid go?

Running away can't become a regular occurrence. He's one of five kids, and I'm just one person. Julia Caroline can't be around every waking moment. I'm tough, but I'm not cut out for hunting for missing children every day.

I call out for him again and swallow hard. He must be hiding. Why do kids love playing hide and go seek so much?

"Sweetie, you're scaring me. Please come out from wherever you're hiding."

Rounding the corner of the potting shed, I see him sitting on the bench Wesley built for me when he was in high school. Wesley and I used to have picnics out here in the summer because it was so cool under the thick natural canopy created by all the oak trees. I'd forgotten how special this spot was to us until now.

How did Clint find it? I've never seen him wander this far from the house. Maybe Wesley showed it to him at some point.

I rub my temples to soothe a tension headache. "Hey, honey. Why did you run out of the house? Were you upset to see your mama and daddy on the TV? I'm sorry. I want you to see videos and pictures of them. It's okay to be sad."

Clint shakes his head. "No. I saw Mama."

"Honey, I know. Maybe it was too soon to show y'all those videos. I'm so sorry. We'll have to put the videos away for a while."

"No, Nana! Mama—she's right here. Look!" He points to a cluster of trees just beyond the bench, and I see the faint glowing outline of a slender woman's body. Stepping closer, I can make out long, flowing brown curls and a sweet smile.

I fall to my knees. Indeed—it's MaryAnne. I can't believe it! As she approaches me, I can't hold back my tears. This can't be real. Thank you, Lord, for bringing my boys' sweet mama back.

MaryAnne bends down to hug me, and I don't want to let go. I never knew you could feel an embrace from a spirit, but it's like she has never left this world.

The rose bushes in my garden smell sweeter than they have in months, and the air is lighter. Life seems almost normal.

When MaryAnne lets go, I wipe the tears from my face and stand. "Child, I can't possibly explain how much we've all missed you and Wesley. You were an angel who walked this earth. Everyone who ever met you said so, and I had the great honor of having you as my daughter-in-love—the selfless person who put my son and your darling children first in everything you did."

Clint runs up to me and wraps his arms around my waist, and I try not to cry again. No wonder he didn't want to break his promise about the secret! As adamant as he was, I should have known the request came from his mama.

MaryAnne flashes her trademark radiant grin. "I know our boys are in the right place with you. You love them as much as we do, and you'll always keep their best interests at heart. Wesley wishes he could be here, but it wasn't possible this time."

My eyes dart from Clint's wrinkled forehead to MaryAnne. "Can you help us understand how this works?"

"I wish. We haven't gotten this whole visiting earth thing down to a science quite yet. Sometimes, I can make myself appear and even move things or...um...people.

I gasp. "So, you got me out of the house when it was burning all by yourself? How?" My hands tremble—I can't see how she managed to move me alone.

"Oh, I had some help. Something clicked for Wesley that day, and he held back the flames while I walked with Clint over to Julia Caroline's house. I came back as soon as I knew he was safe to watch over you and the other children. We pulled you out of the house right after you collapsed, but we could only get you to the porch before the first firetruck got there."

I shake my head. "Well, I'll be. You saved my life." I can't muster saying anything else.

MaryAnne smiles. "I'm so glad everything fell into place for us that day. What's scary is sometimes, I'm lucky to make it here at all. Wesley is having even less success, despite your mama showing us a few tricks she has up her sleeve. It was her idea to write you the notes and put them in the charm. It takes less energy for us to write the notes than to show ourselves."

My mind is going a million miles a second with questions. I couldn't possibly ask them all, so I settle for the obvious. "Will you and Wesley be able to come back again? What about my mama? Will y'all still send us notes?"

She shrugs. "I sure hope so. We all do. No matter what, we will always watch over y'all. We love you. Thank you for cherishing and protecting our boys. Don't forget to live your life, too." She gestures toward the garden gate. Brian waves and lets himself in the backyard.

Everything slows down as I consider what MaryAnne said. I can't cling to the life we used to have. All I've wanted since the accident was to see Wesley and MaryAnne again.

Now, that I've seen her and know more regular visits are possible, my heart feels a little less empty. It's not the same as having her and Wesley around every day, living their rich full lives as parents and contributing members of our tight-knit community. But it's something. The boys and I are building a new life together, and from the looks of things, Brian wants to be part of it.

MaryAnne blows a kiss to us and begins fading in a silvery mist. I hug Clint as we watch her disappear. His face falls, taking my heart with it.

I squeeze him tight. "Are you alright, honey?"

He looks upward and nods. "Yeah. Mama had to get back to Heaven. That's her home now."

Wisdom out of the mouth of babes—Clint is right. The angel who once walked this earth now spends most of her time in Heaven. Although it's heartbreaking to not have her with us every day, I can't think of a more deserving person to live in Paradise.

I'm thankful for the blessings from above, the five little ones who call me Nana, and the second chance to get things right with Brian. Our story is just beginning.

Also by Stephanie Edwards

The Haunting on Palm Court: An Isle of Palms Suspense #1

Return to Palm Court: An Isle of Palms Suspense #2

Christmas on Palm Court: An Isle of Palms Suspense #3

The Word Dancer: An Appalachian Tale

Check out music by

in the Palm Court book trailers on YouTube and on your favorite music services.

www.ingramcontent.com/pod-product-compliance
Lightning Source LLC
Chambersburg PA
CBHW060454300726
48975CB00008B/2517